Stay Connected with Us!

Text **LOCKDOWN** to 22828 to stay up-to-date with new releases, sneak peaks, contests and more…

Like our page on Facebook:
Lock Down Publications

Join Lock Down Publications/The New Era Reading Group

Visit our website:
www.lockdownpublications.com

Follow us on Instagram:
Lock Down Publications

Email Us: We want to hear from you!

Chapter 1

Deep in the heart of this untamed medium security prison. 9:30 a.m.

I was outside on the crowded courtyard, walking laps, listening to my own thoughts. Not all of the time is that a good thing because I can be a bit of a maniac at times and not get along with myself. Hey, I'm just being honest. But on that fine morning, me versus me was good. The only reason I was outside that early was because my cellmate needed some alone time in the cell. My choices were to sit out in the dayroom and listen to the guys lust over whatever female Daytime talk show host that was on the TV at the time, or go out on the courtyard. I chose the courtyard because it was just way too early to deal with their level of perversion.

While outside, I quietly walked laps, minding my own business. Then I observed a small group of guys giving me hard stares.

Just when I was telling myself that I was just trippin' and it was all in my head, this white boy walked up on me and whispered for me to be on guard, then just walked off. Hell! I don't even think he ever stopped moving, now that I think about it. Now I ain't new to this. I got about ten calendars in and I'm from the streets, so I'm always on point. Still, I wondered why he felt the need to warn me. It wasn't until my homie—Trey-9—pulled me aside that I found out that this

Lock Down Publications and Ca$h
Presents

FO'EVA ROLLIN'

Choices Made, Consequences Paid

Written By
Assa Raymond Baker

Copyright © 2024 Assa Raymond Baker
FO'EVA ROLLIN'

All rights reserved. No part of this book may be reproduced in any form or by electronic or mechanical means, including information storage and retrieval systems without permission in writing from the publisher, except by a reviewer who may quote brief passages in review.

First Edition 2024

Printed in the United States of America

This is a work of fiction. Names, characters, places, and incidents either are products of the author's imagination or are used fictitiously. Any similarity to actual events or locales or persons, living or dead, is entirely coincidental.

Lock Down Publications
P.O. Box 944
Stockbridge, GA 30281
www.lockdownpublications.com

Like our page on Facebook: Lock Down Publications
www.facebook.com/lockdownpublications.ldp

young fool ass nigga was plotting to extort me and talkin' shit with a few others 'bout running up in my cell on me.

This wasn't new info to me. I'd been hearing the goofy talk his shit 'bout me for a while, but said nothin' to him because I'd made a promise to my youngest daughter to stay outta trouble. Also, I was in the midst of finishing up an anthology of erotic short stories that my publisher couldn't wait to get his hands on. I don't know what came over me, but that morning I'd just had enough of his bullshit. I knew he couldn't do anything with me one-on-one, and could see that they wasn't tryna do anything out in the open. So, I promptly excused myself from Trey-9, not letting 'im know what I was about to do, and marched over to where the young goofy was standing with the small group of guys that I'd observed watching me when I walked out, and pulled his hoe card right there in front of everyone.

Afterwards, I nonchalantly sauntered back inside the building, heading straight on to my cell. I reached my cell without any incident.

By that time, my cellmate had been long gone, so I was in there all alone waiting with a pair of brown-cloth workman's gloves on, ready for them to make good on the promise to run up in there on the thug. Shid, I grew up in a hood where we jumped each other for fun, so I was looking to have a good time.

Knowing that I'd left all eyes on the goofy, I should've known that in order to save face he would show up by his lonesome. So, I'm standing on the far side of the room with my back against the wall and my arms folded across my chest when my cell door is ripped open, but the goofy ass niggah don't come inside. Instead, he starts talkin' stupid, tryna get me to follow him someplace else to box. The fool had the nerve to say that he ain't tryna go to the Hole. Note, I'm not a lil guy. I'm 5'11", 225 pounds solid, and can damn near lift double my body weight, just to give you an idea of what this 185lbs, maybe 190lbs, 5'8" sloppy-built goofy put himself up against. I'm not the baddest niggah, but I got hands fo'real.

I informed the dumb-ass that no matter what, we're going to the Hole, because I'm not gonna play fight with him. Seeing that he wasn't about to advance, I walked over to him and told him to get the fuck away from my cell and to keep my name out his mouth. I guess he had to play tough and put on a show for the small audience below us in the dayroom that was watching him, because the goofy responded, "Bitch, if you want it you know how to start a fight." I'm known to be a spontaneous type of guy, so I instantly agreed.

"You right," I retorted, then promptly fed 'im a hard three-piece special that made his eyes cross. I was impressed that the goofy didn't drop and a bit surprised when he shook it off and got right to work. He threw a slow hard right that I easily blocked. I fed him a couple stiff jabs to think about. He staggered back a bit, then rushed me wildly, swinging both hands. I blocked a few and ate a few before I commenced to giving him the ass whoopin' that his daddy should've gave him long ago.

While we were trading blows, he grabbed me by the shoulder and dragged me down the tier until we were in front of one of his guy's cells. Once he had me there, he started bumpin' up against the door. I guess he was lookin' fo' help. Well, outta the corner of my eye, I saw a shadow appear in the window of the cell. My dumbass looked in its direction and got hit in the mouth hard enough to knock my tooth loose. That pissed me the fuck off and I let him know it. I started hitting him harder and harder. He couldn't take it, so he grabbed me.

I ain't with that hugging shit. But when I snatched away from him, I somehow lost my footing and stumbled backwards. He saw this and immediately rushed me. This time I grabbed him and took 'im down to the floor with me. As soon as my back hit the ground, I put him in my half guard and we grappled. He was trying his hardest not to allow me to lock him in a chokehold, but wasn't strong enough to stop me. Just as I got the hold locked, the unit officer ran over.

"Stop fighting!" he bellowed, but we did not stop. "I got spray!" he warned us. I knew what that meant, so I pushed goofy up and ducked my head into his chest, using him for a shield. He got hit with the most of it. He jumped off the ground screaming and floppin' around like he'd been set on fire. Yeah, that's how the spray feels, but I'm not with all of that screaming and cryin' shit.

I stood up and considered running over to finish punishing him. But then there were two officers suddenly in between us and I didn't want that type of charge. Not thinking, I blinded myself by wiping my eyes in attempt to keep the spray out of 'em. My gloves were soaked with the stuff, so it defeated the purpose. Feeling like a fool, I allowed the officers to walk me down the stairs and sit me at a table in the dayroom. The dayroom was now empty because they'd made everyone lock down in their cells. I could still hear the goofy hollering and screaming, which is why I think they hurried up and took him out to the Restrictive Housing Unit, also known as the Hole.

Now, my macho man shit was wearing thin, no lie. It seems like the longer I sat there covered in that spray, the more painful the burning got. I asked the officers as calmly as I could if they would allow me to rinse my face in the sink. My request was denied. They stated that it would only make it worse. So now I'm thinking, *how in the fuck do they make it stop if water makes it worse*. I don't know how long I sat waiting for the van to return to take me to RHU, but I can tell you I ain't never been as glad as I was then to be tossed in back of a patrol car and taken to lock up. As soon as I got there, the first thing they did was lock me in a shower stall and told me to wash the spray off. I knew them muthafuckas was on some bullshit when they told me the water would make it worse. But, in a way, they were right because the showers are a preset temperature, and the hot water surely didn't make it better. I had to step out from under the water and catch water in my hands to clear my eyes with. The hot water burned my skin too badly for me to step back under the water once I'd gotten my eyesight back, so I abandoned the idea. I dried myself, then dressed in the clean clothes that I'd been given—an orange T-shirt, socks, underwear and pants.

Once dressed, I was placed in a holding cell where I was photoed before being taken out to the hospital in town to have my tooth reset. The two officers who escorted me to the hospital got me there quickly and in one piece. They were even kind enough to get me a wheelchair to ride in instead of forcing me to walk in the shiny handcuffs and shackles that I was sporting for our outing.

Inside, they parked me in front of the check-in window. The nurse looked up at me and gave me a pretty smile. She held eye contact with me long enough for me to believe she was flirting, and the sudden color in her checks had me wondering, *was this a part of one of her secret fantasies*? But I said nothing more than I had to, to get myself checked into the hospital. Don't get me wrong, she was sexy. She stood about 5'9", with highlighted brunette tresses that hugged her flawless face before stopping just past her shoulders. She dressed in a short, dark purple top with skin-tight black pants that showed her camel-toe that made wonder how was she allowed to wear them to work. I kept my eyes on her the whole time she made her way out from behind the window to come place a band on my left wrist. She could've put it on me through the window but she wanted me to get a good look at her; I could tell by the way she made a show of placing the band on me. She had positioned herself in front of me so that I got a clear view down her shirt. Hey, I've been down ten long years, hell yeah, I looked. She had enough tits to make the black Victoria Secret bra look amazing on her. She caught me lookin' and widened her smile, then caressed my face as she went out of her way to put a yellow COVID mask over my nose and mouth.

After that, I was taken into the waiting room. Not long after, the pain from my mouth got so bad my eyes watered, which made them burn once again from the leftover spray that was clearly still on me. Blinded again, I immediately informed the officers and they quickly went and retrieved the sexy nurse who'd checked me in. She took me to an eye-rinse station that I had to revisit twice more before leaving the hospital. Anyways, back in the waiting room, another nurse, not as good lookin' as the first one, came and took me to my room. There, my blood pressure was checked, and all of that good stuff. Then I had to wait for them to come in and do some x-rays. After that, a small medical team came in the room, and checked out the injuries to my mouth.

One of the male doctors ordered the nurse to give me a pain blocker, then they left the room. I was so happy to hear him tell her to do that, man. A few minutes later, the nurse returned with the longest damn needle in the world, it seemed. I'm not afraid of gettin' shots, but it was something about that needle that held my attention. I think it bothered me 'cause it was supposed to go into my mouth. And into my mouth it did. It hurt like hell too. But shortly after it was done and the nurse had gone, my whole face numbed and I couldn't feel a thing.

For about a half-hour, I sat up in bed watching the animated movie, *Trolls*, with the two officers. The movie was interesting and funny, to be honest. Well, just before the ending of the movie, the team of medical staff returned. The same doctor that had ordered the pain blocker shot reset my tooth and covered it with some goop to hold it in place, then ordered the nurse to hold it until it dried. So for the next five minutes or so, I had this woman with her fingers in my mouth watchin' the ending of *Trolls* with us. When the goop had set, I was discharged and taken back to the prison and tossed back in the Restrictive Housing Unit to await my hearing.

Chapter 2

Morning of July 7, 2022.

    I was awakened from my restless slumber by the sound of the officer knockin' on the cell door with his key. When I acknowledged him, he informed me that he was there to take me to hear my conduct report. I was still dressed from breakfast, so I rolled out of bed, slipped on my shoes, then went over to the sink and freshened up. Once I was ready, I made my way over to the door and shoved my hands through the tray opening. The officer slapped handcuffs on me, making sure I was nice and secured before opening the door.
    I was escorted into a small cluttered room where two captains sat behind a computer. After I'd been sat down and tethered to the floor across from the messy desk, the captains introduced themselves. The one seated in front of the computer tapped a few keys on the keyboard, then went through a few preliminaries before he began.
    "At approximately 10:20 a.m., on July 2nd, 2022, while on my assigned post as the Unit A officer, I, C/O Pomes, noticed 2 inmates fighting on the upper left tier. I communicated on the radio that there was a fight on Unit A, and proceeded to close the dayroom down. Sgt. McSay then arrived on the wing to assist with closing down the dayroom. I went up the stairs to address the situation. As I approached the 2 inmates, I observed both inmates engaged in physical activity as they were throwing closed fist punches at each

other, which had caused blood to be visible on the floor of the tier. I gave the directive to '*stop fighting*'. I gave this directive three times. After the 3rd time, I announced that I had pepper spray." The inmates still continued to wrestle on the ground and throw punches at each other's faces and bodies. At this time, I deployed a 1-second burst-on target to the 2 fighting inmates. I then directed the inmates to stop fighting, at which this time they complied. Staff arrived on scene to apply restraints and escort the inmates to RHU. Let it be known that the 2 inmates involved in the fight were inmate Baker, A. and inmate Knight, F. I observed physical injuries to both inmates' facial areas. The spill kit was used due to blood on the floor from the inmates' facial wounds/cuts. Photos of scene, inmates and video footage, accompany this report as evidence." He finished reading, then asked, "How does that sound to you?"

"It's what happened," I replied.

"How do you plead?"

"Guilty. I did it, ain't no need to play and drag it out."

"Okay, since you're handling this today, I'm going to drop the Disruptive Conduct since it as due to the fight and find you guilty of Assault and Disobeying orders. Here, you do half time and since we know you're not a troublemaker I'm going to give you thirty days, in which you will serve fifteen days if you do not get anymore conduct reports while you're here in seg!" he finished. The other captain called for the officer to come escort me back to my cell.

Once back in my cell, I decided—since I was up—to do my workout. ". . . ninety-seven . . . ninety-eight . . . ninety-nine . . . hundred!" I bellowed, thereafter taking a walk to catch my breath.

"Aye, OG? Aye, OG!"

"Wuddup?" I responded to the voice coming through the air vent.

"I hear you gettin' it in over there and shit."

"Yeah, I try to keep it together."

"Yeah, if I didn't know you were over in that cell by yo'self, I'd swear you were over there jackin' for some hoes, doing sets of a hundred an' shit."

"Naw, I'm too old fo' all that. I leave all of that to you youngsters." I chuckled. "If a broad wanna show from me, she gon have to put on one for me."

"I hear that. Talk that shit then!" He laughed. "What you doing anyway? Pushups?"

Now I know he could hear me over here jumpin' around. The nigga was just tryna see if I was gonna lie to him. "Nawl, jumping jacks. I do sets of a hundred of 'em, and sets of fifty of everything else. I usually try to do five hundred of each."

"Damn! That's better than what I be doing over here. I do a thousand pushups in sets of twenty-five, then run in place fo' an hour."

"That's good."

"Not when I'm about to be twenty-five and you're a half of a hundred." He laughed.

"Hey, hey, hey! I ain't that old. I still got a good five years to go. I got a daughter 'bout yo' age who be talkin' that same shit. She be sayin' things like, she gon' push me outta me wheelchair and hide my walker."

"You got a walker?"

"Hell nawl! She just be talkin' crazy because I told her I'ma spank that ass when I catch her." I chuckled at the memory of that conversation with my daughter.

"You know the only time I've seen you was when they took you to the shower," he explained, then asked, "Aye, what they call you, OG?"

"AR-40." I lied, using the name of my character in the book that I'm currently working on.

"AR-40," he repeated. "I ain't ever heard of you befo', but then again I ain't been here that long either. They call me Duke."

"You wouldn't have because I don't be out there like that. Just like I don't be doing all of this talkin' through the vent shit usually."

"OG man, I'm glad you talkin' to me. I'm goin' crazy in this bitch. I can't use the phone, get my TV, tablet, no nothin'. This shit crazy!"

"Lil' bro, you can't let this lil' shit here break you, at least not like that. If you don't like this shit, get out and stay out. That goes fo' both this Hole and prison. What you do to get put in here anyway?" I inquired, taking a seat onto the stainless steel sink and toilet combo so I can talk closer to the vent without yelling.

"Man, that shit crazy!" he exclaimed. "Man, I had to touch my celly up 'cause the niggah stole my wife email address outta my tablet. Like, she wasn't gonna check with me first befo' she accepted it. When I asked him what was up, why he do it, he tried to give me some lame ass reason 'bout just in case somethin' happen to me. If somethin' happened to me, then the niggah could just email her from my tablet. So on that I got boogie with 'im."

"I take it, *got boogie*, means y'all fought? You know I'm old, you can't just be sayin' stuff and using terms I ain't ever heard used in a way befo'," I said and we laughed. I shared with him what happened to get me tossed in the box. That's when he found out my true identity. He told me that he had heard about the incident.

"Man OG, these niggahs here crazy. I ain't no punk or nothin' but it's too many niggahs that got love fo' you fo' me to try something that stupid. My niggah—Solid—can't wait 'til that niggah get out so he can get at 'im for the disrespect. Everybody said that you handled yo' business, but bro nem still heated behind it!" he explained. "So you be writing them books?"

"Yeah. It's a stress release and a way for me to take my mind off of this hell we're living in. Have you ever read any of my books?"

"Not yet, but Solid put me up on 'em and I had my wife order 'em for me. She got Amazon Prime, so she downloaded *Cash In, Cash Out* 1&2 off Amazon and loved them. I told her ass to wait 'til I get the books so we can read 'em together and talk about them."

"Awwwh!" I teased him.

"Fuck you!" he retorted. We both laughed.

"Aye, when you talk to her tell her to leave an honest review about 'em. And tell her to look up my other books that's released under Assa Reigns and to cop *W.I.F.E* 1&2, by Raneissa Baker."

"Hell yeah. She gon' trip when I tell her I'm in here kickin' it with you!" he said excitedly. It always feels good to get praise for my work. My favorite part is when people try to get me to tell them who the real people are that my stories are based on. "Hey, OG?"

"Wuddup?"

"Tell me what ol' AR-40 was on out in the world."

"On like what?"

"You know, like how back in the day when you were out there trappin' and poppin' bottles with hoes an' shit."

"You know what, Duke? I'ma do this fo' you. Fuck it. Since the subject of the day seems to be 'bout hoe ass niggahs, I'ma keep going with that. But Duke, yo' ass better listen 'cause I'm not finna be keep repeating myself." I took a sip of water then cleared my throat and began . . .

Chapter 3

My sister—Alexis—lives on the West coast in Seattle. She's heavy into music, she's nice with producing beats. She's known as DJ Lexi and is one of the hottest DJs out there. In fact, her talent for making beats is how she met and fell in love with a nice up and coming rap artist named King Tivon. A mutual friend of theirs had recommended her to King Tivon who, at the time, was working on a new album and looking for a new sound to flow to. My sister eagerly agreed to make the trip down to LA to work with the hot underground artist that she'd been bumpin' in her club mixes.

"Damn, Lexi, you're hotter than I expected!" King Tivon blurted out when he greeted Alexis. "I'm—"

"King Tivon. Come on, now do you really think that you need to introduce yourself. I know who you are. I spin your songs in a lot of my mixes."

"That's wussup! Everyone I fuck with calls me KT and since we're going to be spending a lil' time together, please feel free to call me the same," he said, lightly shaking her hand while staring into her eyes. "Lexi, I don't mean to make things weird but I need to say this—Your IG pics caught you. I'm mean it, they stayed true to your beauty."

"Thank you!" she said, smiling. Falling in love was the farthest thing from Lexi's mind. She went to the studio hoping that he would be her way into the area of the music business where she could make the big bucks, but when they laid eyes on one another, the sparks between them were almost instant.

They worked late into the night, long after the others with them had called it a night, leaving the two of them alone. They passionately went back and forth tweaking each other's work, making one hot track after another. During the times when KT stood in the booth listening to his playback, he could not keep his eyes off Lexi's light, creamy, peanut butter tone face, or the nice cleavage. He noticed that another top button on her shirt had popped open, and a good portion of her full breasts was visible every time she leaned forward or did her lil' happy dance in her seat.

When they took a break to replenish their bodies with food, Lexi learned that they were both born in Milwaukee, Wisconsin. She also learned that they had both moved away when they were young kids; him to Chicago, Illinois, and her to Seattle, Washington. They had so many things in common, and their attraction was so strong that lil' sis felt like they were meant to be. At the end of the meal, she had her mind made up that if he moved on her, she would ride the wave of the vibe that she was feeling. With that set in mind, Lexi excused herself to go to the ladies' room.

KT couldn't help staring at her plump ass as she sashayed away. If sis would have looked back and caught him ogling her, he had no intention on apologizing for looking, but she had the best looking natural butt he had seen in a long time. When Lexi returned to the table, there was another button open on her shirt, exposing more of her breasts. As they resumed their conversation, King Tivon produced a bottle of Tequila. Before long, the two of them were feeling no pain.

King Tivon put his hand on Lexi's knee, and kissed her while working on opening the remaining few buttons of her top. She gave herself to the kiss and allowed him to do what he was doing even after her shirt fell open. She twirled her fingers in his long locs, allowing him to slowly slide his hand up her thigh and under her skirt. She didn't even try to resist as he pushed her knees apart so he had easy access to her garden. She moaned encouragingly as KT's fingers began dipping in her wetness, playing with her clit.

Lexi spread her legs farther apart, hanging them over the arms of the black soft leather chair that she sat in as KT slipped between her thighs. She eagerly peeled him out of his shirt as he pushed his jeans and boxers down to his knees. As soon as she felt his hardness slap against her belly, she reached down, grabbed it and aimed it at her tight opening. KT happily pushed inside her while sucking on her throat. Lexi squealed as he filled her with his hard length, and pulled her knees up to her chest so he can give it all to her. She was so wet that in no time KT was pounding her so hard that the seat was creaking, threatening to break from the force.

Lexi squealed loudly with every hard stroke as he sawed in and out. When she started pushing her depth up to meet him, KT grunted that he was going to shoot, and plowed his length all the way inside her until his balls slapped her ass. When she came for the second time, she felt his tip swell and his body jerk, and knew that he was about to climax. She quickly pulled him out of her and stroked him with her hand until he shot gob after gob of nut all over her tight fist.

From that night the two of them were inseparable. About three months into their relationship, sis learned that King Tivon had his ways, but what young rich niggah didn't? She was in love, so she looked past his mood swings and neediness. Another three months or so into their relationship after one of her DJ sets, they were on their way to Lexis' house and got into an argument over something really minor. They had both been drinking, so she blew it off when he slammed her against the car by her throat.

The following day, KT informed sis about a couple of shows that he got booked to do in Milwaukee and asked her to come with him. She said yeah right away without a second thought. Just like with me, we've both been waiting to reconnect, but hell, life just kept gettin' in the way of us making it happen. I'm the oldest. I got two sisters and two brothers, so it's only fair that I take most of the blame for it. As many times that I'd been out West, I could've looked them up but I was always too busy tryna dodge these prison cells to do so.

As soon as Alexis made it to Milwaukee, she immediately got in touch with her mother's side of the family, which are the well-known Love family. She wasn't very close to our father's side of the family nor our father. Hell, she didn't even know until like three years after that the he'd died of a heart attack and I was the one who had to give 'em the bad news. Alexis is built the way most of the women are paying top dollar to be built, and the way that most of them hot IG models that's plastered across many of the prison cell walls are built. So you can use your imagination from that. Since Alexis and I are half-siblings, Ty don't consider me her family. It's her way of dealing with the crazy crush she has on me.

Man, it wasn't until her and sis hooked that she even knew that I was Alexis' big brother. Tyneil is the reason my sis was able to get back in touch with me in the first place, because I'd lost all of my contact info when my phone was taken in a robbery of one of my trap-houses, but that's another story. Yeah, I'm a Brew City banger to the core. There's not a hood that I can't step foot in on the city's North side. Now the South side is a different story. There's a whole different breed of people over there; it's almost like being in two different cities. On the North, the hoods are cliquish because it's 'bout money and the power. But on the South, they gangbang, 'cause it's about a name and fear in their hoods. I can still go over there, but I don't press my luck. I used to get money over there back in the early 90s but then the gangbanging became too much for me once the MP-13s popped up on the scene.

I don't really trap in the Mil like that though. Yeah, there's a few family members and true thugs whose hands I hit with a lil wurk, but not many. It's just too much work for me to get money on the streets of my city. That's why I hit the road and hustle up in the northern parts of the state where the gettin' is good.

Chapter 4

On the day Alexis arrived, I was up in Appleton, Wisconsin kickin' it with my guys—Chese and Lil Dave. I ain't gon' lie, them two having it their way up there. I mean they're like gods to them niggahs that surround 'em; of course whenever I pop up on the scene, I receive the same welcome. On that day though, I wasn't there to hang out. Chese had just coped some soft white wurk from me and needed me to put it together for 'im.

'Bout to double up and bubble up / She ain't fuckin', we'll wish her luck / A quarter bird in a dually truck. You ain't never had to scoop it up / A niggah lost it all, had to pick it up / A hundred round with a coolant touch / A nigah hit it, it's a touch and bust..." I was in the kitchen of his spot bobbing my head and rapping along to Starlito's hit song, *Brick Music*, while standing over the stove water whippin' up a fo' and a split for cuzo when I received a call from an unknown number. I sent it to voicemail, then texted the number askin' that the unknown caller text me 'cause it's too loud where I was to talk.

A few moments later, I received a text that read: *Hey there big brother! This Lexi. I'm here in Milwaukee and tryna kick it with you while I'm here. This my number hit me back. Love you, Miss you!* I almost responded back and asked who in the fuck is Lexi, but as soon as the thought filled my mind it hit me that it was my lil' sister. I instantly stopped what I was doing and went outside in the quiet of the night and called her back.

"Damn, bro, it sho got quiet where you at fast," she said, answering the call on the first ring.

"What the fuck, sis! How long you been here? I mean *there*, because I'm not in the city right now!" I excitedly inquired.

"I just got here early this morning. My guy gotta perform at a couple of clubs, so I'll be here for a couple of days. I'm really wanting to see you while I'm here though."

"Shid, I'm still in the state. I'll be there in no later than about two hours."

"That's wussup! I'ma text you the address of the club that he's doing the show at. If you don't make it here before we leave to go there, just come there. I'll tell 'em to let you in."

"That'll work even better. I'll see you soon." I heard a female's voice in the background telling sis to ask me did I miss her too. "Sis, who that with you talkin' 'bout do I miss her?"

"Bro, that's Tyneil ass."

"Tyneil?"

"Yeah, Tyneil AR. Don't act like you don't know me!"

"Oh, damn! How y'all know each other, Ty?"

"Lexi my cousin. How come you never told me that she's your sister?"

"Ty, you answer that question yo'self. Yo ass sittin' there talkin' like we fuck with each other the long way an' shit. I didn't have a reason to share none of my personal family info with you."

"You would if you quit playin' and let me have yo' babies," she retorted, giggling.

"Girl, stop. The only thing you wanna do is swallow my babies. Don't try an' front for my sister." I chuckled. "Anyway, all that shit dead fo'real now that I know we're family."

"You and her family, not you and me. Y'all don't got the same mama and her mama is my auntie, so that makes us nothing to each other. So if you ask me I'll say yes."

"Sis, I'll see you later, promise. I'ma get up off this phone 'cause I ain't got time fo' Ty's mess right now." As I was ending the call I heard Tyneil say something about me makin' her chase me and shook my head.

Rushing back inside the spot, I found Chese and Lil Dave lost in a heavy cloud of weed smoke. I told 'em what's up with my long lost sister suddenly popping up down in the Mil and that I was leaving. They understood and actually contemplated going back with me, but somebody had to stay back to get all that paper that was flowing through there. So they stayed and I finished up in the kitchen, then jumped in my trusty Ford Crown Victoria and floated comfortably on gleaming chrome 22-inch rims all of the way down to the Mil.

Once at the crib, I had to get myself together. Hell, I ain't seen my little sister since she was like eight years old, and she was twenty-seven now. So hell yeah I had to look my best. I didn't need to shave because I'd hit the barber shop earlier that day, so I showered, dressed and hit the door. I chose my Camaro to drive to the club where she was at. It's not that anyone of my other whips wouldn't have been good enough to drive there, 'cause, real talk, all my rides are head turners. I drove the Camaro because at the time its wet black and gold candy paint job went well with my outfit. Ya know a niggah was out there doing the money dance and let it show dressed in Gucci down to the boots. My neck and both wrists were icy as Lake Michigan in the middle of winter. When I stepped in the spot like always, the sack-chasing broads were on me. My mind was on gettin' up with lil' sister. But that didn't stop my BM from catching my eye. She was sitting at the bar with one of her friends and two dudes. Everything about the scene looked like she was on a double date or something.

Now I'm not the jealous type. In truth, I think jealousy is a childish emotion and I'm so grown. If I had to put a label on the relationship I share with Rhonda, I guess you could call it an open one. We see whoever we wanna see but never place anyone before each other. Knowing she would be hot with me if I didn't come over and acknowledge her, I made my way over. She was looking sexy as always, with her long micro braids falling loose over her exposed shoulders. She was dressed in a short firm-fitting black dress, a pair of gold patent leather Jimmy Choo sandals, and several icy gold tennis bracelets had her left wrist sparkling. The only piece of jewelry that I was concerned with was the simple diamond ring that I'd put on her finger.

When I arrived, she was all smiles as introductions were made. I'd been right; she was out on a date. I was player about it and bought 'em all fresh drinks. After telling Rhonda about Alexis being there, I wandered off into the crowd. I wanted to try to pick her out on my own, which wasn't hard because Tyneil's horny ass was right beside her, snapping pictures with a few of her fans. I briskly marched up behind my sister, wrapped my arms around her waist, and lifted her off her feet.

"Heeey, big head!" I said, spinning her around before placing her back down.

"Oh my God! Oh my God, bro!" she screamed, hugging me and crying happy tears.

"If it wasn't for Ty, I wouldn't have recognized you," I admitted. Now I haven't seen my sis in years but I know she had to have told her man that I was meeting 'em at the club, because why wouldn't she? Truthfully, I didn't know what type of woman that Alexis had grown up into, but I do know that she was not foolish enough to be hugging all up on another niggah at an event that her man is the guest of honor at. And I know, at least I thought I knew, ol' King Tivon knew the same about his girl.

But before I knew it, King Tivon had suddenly appeared and without the slightest inquiry he backhanded Alexis and snatched her by her arm so fast that the force of it lifted her off her feet almost as high as I did when I hugged her. Sis screamed out of shock and pain. In that moment I didn't care who the fuck the niggah was, I went right into action. Before Alexis could get her balance together and realize what was going on, I was feeding KT jab after jab after hard jab, each one snapping his head back, making him look like the fool he was fo' being so stupid. Then I slammed his head down on the table not far from where my babymama and her date was sitting.

Rhonda whipped her gun out of her bag and pointed it in the faces of King Tivon's two flunkies who'd rushed over to his aid. I drew my burner and pressed it hard into his ribcage.

"AR, no, don't!" Alexis said, rushing up to us. "He didn't mean it he—"

"Back the fuck up, Lexi!" I snapped at her while pressing her man's face harder onto the tabletop. Sis stopped right where she was. Standing there watching me with fear in her eyes. I got in KT's face and said, "Niggah, you's a stupid muthafucka thinking you can put hands on my sister in front of me. You gotta be a fool if you think she'd disrespect you in your presence. Bitch, the only reason you're still breathin' is because of where we're at and that my little sister says you're drunk." I picked up his head and slammed it down again. "If you ever in yo' life hit her again, niggah, I will kill you. That's a promise."

"Babe, the niggah sorry. Let him go and get outta here before the police come. You know one of these muthafuckas called 'em!" Rhonda said, snapping me out of my building rage. I knew she was speaking the truth, so I let him go but kept my gun out as I backed out of the door.

"I'll call y'all and let ya know I'm good," I told her and sis, then went on out the door. Alexis wasn't that stupid in love with the niggah. She knew that it wasn't gonna be good for her if she stayed there with King Tivon after how I'd treated him. So she collected her purse and followed out behind me.

"Bitch, where you think you going? If you leave with that niggah, we're done!" King Tivon shouted behind her.

"Nigga, we were done when you thought it was smart to put yo' hands on me like I'm a dog out here in front of all of these people and my big brother! Fuck you!" Alexis yelled at him, then rushed out to catch up with me.

I'd just put my gun up in my stash spot just in case someone gave the police my plate number when I spotted Alexis run outside with her things in her hands. The way that she was scanning the cars told me that she was searching for me. I hurriedly spun the car around to her side of the street and pushed the door open for her.

"Lexi, get in!" I exclaimed, getting her attention. She quickly dropped in the passenger seat and closed the door. I pulled off, then glanced at her and saw her looking back at the club. "Sis, I'm not finna apologize fo' what I did. Fuck that punk! I promise you on our Daddy's grave, if I ever find out that he put his hands on you again I'ma kill him."

"I know you will, big brother. I'm done with him. I can't believe he did that to me in front of you and everybody." Her phone started ringing in her purse. When she retrieved it, she looked at the screen and sent the call to voicemail. "This him callin' now," she confessed.

"Listen, I know this isn't his first time puttin' his hands on you. Just like I know you ain't done fuckin' with 'im yet."

"See, that's where you're wrong. I'm so done with his sorry ass. I'd been thinking about leaving him for a while now and he knew it. That's why he asked me to come on this trip with him. His ass knew that I wasn't gonna be there when he got back. I always told myself that if my big brother was with me nothing would be happening to me the way it has been. Now I know it's true!" she explained, resting her head on the headrest. "Aye, who was that girl with the gun?"

"That's Rhonda, my kids' mother. Since you're with me right now we're gonna go meet up with her and her friends. But first, I need to switch out cars just in case the police looking fo' this one!" I said after reading Rhonda's text telling me that she'd left the club. I headed straight out to my storage unit to swop out the Camaro for my cherry-red Yukon.

Chapter 5

Sometimes I'm so damn smart that I'm stupid. Alexis and I met up with Rhonda at her crib. She was at home because the guy she was out with didn't like the fact that she carried a gun and wasn't afraid to use it, so his lame ass bounced. My BM didn't want to be a third wheel on her friend, so she went home and texted me to see if I was okay.

"I'm good, Luv," I said when she answered my call. I'd just swopped out the Camaro for the Yukon and was heading back on our side of town. I hate texting and driving, so I called her back.

"How about your sister? How is she?"

"She okay," I answered, glancing over at sis who was typing away on her phone. "She wants to meet you. I know you like to go eat after you've been out drinkin' so I figure we can come hang out with y'all, that's if you didn't have other plans?"

"Ain't no, y'all. It's just me at home by my lonesome. When you made me pull my gun on the fools—"

"Whoa, I didn't make you do nothin' like that."

"Assa, you did because you know I wasn't about to let them niggahs run up on you. So yeah, niggah, you made me do it."

"Okay, I'll accept that." I chuckled. "So what happened after I left?"

"The dude Kim's man hooked me up with started talking shit about me having a gun, and a bunch of craziness about what his woman can and can't do, so I told him to kick rocks and came home."

"Are you still dressed?"

"Yeah, why?"

"I'm finna come get you so we can go get somethin' to eat and you can meet Lexi officially. I feel she can use another woman's wisdom right now away."

"Well, hurry up and get here. Just so you know, you're coming home with me afterwards. Seeing you the way you were in the club got my juices flowing."

"I knew you loved the thug in me," I teased, heading to her house while we went back and forth on the phone. It was a kinda foreplay whenever we did this because in the end I've always ended up deep between those big chocolate thighs of hers.

The three of us ended up eating at Denny's since Alexis couldn't go back to her hotel. Plus, she wanted to meet the kids in the morning—or I should say when they got up—because it was already morning. I think it was just after 12 a.m., nope, it was closer to 1:30. I remember it because I'd looked at the clock on the dash when the police pulled us over on the way back to Rhonda's.

This is why I said that I was stupid. We were in the truck just laughin', having ourselves a good ol' time listening to my BM telling stories about me and the kids. All of a sudden, I saw flashing lights speeding toward us in my rearview mirror. I really did think too much of it because I hadn't done anything wrong as far as my driving goes. I assumed that they were just fuckin' with me because of the 28-inch red and chrome rims on my glossy whip, so when they got behind me I pulled right over. Again, I wasn't worried; my burner was locked away in my stash spot behind the in-dash 10" inch screen Sony radio. Rhonda had hers with her, but it was in her bag and registered to her, so like I said I had no worries.

"Could I see your license and insurance please?" the officer asked as soon as I turned on the interior lights and lowered the window for him.

"Yeah, but why you pull us over?" I inquired, moving cautiously to retrieve my wallet from my pocket to give him what he'd asked for.

"Sir, license and insurance please!" he said more aggressively.

"I'm gettin' it for you!" I retorted as I flicked through my insurance cards. Yeah, I made sure that all of mine is legit. "Why you pull us over?" I demanded again, handing him the documents.

"I smell alcohol. Have you been drinking?"

"I don't drink."

"But we do!" Rhonda spoke up. "We had a few drinks tonight at the club, officer. But he doesn't drink or do drugs, nor is it any alcohol in here."

"Can I see your ID, Miss, since you're so full of information?"

"You sure can. Just so you know, I have a loaded firearm in my bag and I have all of my paperwork with me!" she promptly informed the officer.

"Ma'am, I'm going to need you to put your hands where I can see them. Leave your bag where it is. All of you get out of the vehicle nice and slow!" he directed now with his gun in hand.

I didn't say another word. We all just got out of the truck like we were asked. The second officer immediately retrieved Rhonda's bag and placed it on the hood of the truck. He removed her gun, then handed the purse to her so she could get the documents to show proof of the weapon. The first officer immediately placed me in handcuffs. I guess he would rather deal with two black women without the threat of the big black man standing free nearby. I was mad as hell but I didn't say shit. I just let him do what he did, because I say this again, I just knew I was good.

After the second officer let the girls seat back in the truck, he went back to the squad car and ran all of our info, including my license plate to the truck which is registered to me, the same as the Camaro. A few minutes later, I was sitting in back of the squad car under arrest for assault with a deadly weapon. Just like I feared, someone had gotten my license plate number off my car at the club and given it to the police. That gave them reason enough to put a warrant out for me. The officers allowed Rhonda to keep my truck, then hauled me off to jail. Dawg, man, you know how that shit goes. They got seventy-two hours to hold me before I have to be officially charged or let go. I made eye contact with my sister as I was being driven away. She looked sad and hurt. All I could think was, *this was some family reunion.* It's one that'll never be forgotten for sure.

Chapter 6

Later on that day, Rhonda found out that I didn't have a bail and there was nothing that she could do but wait it out, the same way I had to do. She thought it would be a good idea for Alexis to get her things from the motel. By this time, they had hooked up with Tyneil since that's who sis planned to stay with until I got out of jail. Her plan was not to go back home until she knew I would be okay. Sis blamed herself for everything that happened to me and knew the only true way of showing me that my sacrifice wasn't for nothing was for her to stand on her word, and not go back to King Tivon.

Knowing KT, Alexis knew that he would be with his two cousins. The same ones who was with him at the club, and figured that they would be out riding around looking for her, or maybe parked up the street from her grandmother's house waiting for her to come out. King Tivon knew better than to bring any kinda drama to Big Mama Love's house. The fact that KT had stopped callin' and texting sis like crazy made her believe that he was staked out outside of the only place he knew she would go.

Just to be safe, she had Rhonda to drive by her grandmother's crib to see if she could spot the Cadillac Escalade that he'd rented from the airport when they got to Milwaukee. It didn't take any effort for them to spot the Escalade parked at the corner of Mama Love's block. Knowing where King Tivon was, the three women quickly headed to the hotel to get Lexi's bags. Everything went smooth as planned at the hotel. They were in and out with no problems. On the way from the hotel, Rhonda stopped at the gas station to fill up the tank. My uncle—Ed—told me a long time ago that if you treat the halfway mark like it was E, then you'll always have gas when you need it most. I took that jewel and have been running with it ever since. Rhonda followed that same rule.

Anyways, she pulled up to the gas pump closest to the building and all three of them got out. Rhonda put the gas nozzle in the tank and set the little catch thing on the handle as she listened to Tyneil tell the story of how she got into doing porn. Alexis was on the phone explaining everything that had gone down between me, KT and her to her mother.

"Gurl, I love me some good D but damn! I don't know if a bitch can handle as much as you be gettin'." The nozzle snapped off when the tank was full. "Gurl, I'm not tryna get too much in your business, but when I get back I wanna hear about how it was when you fucked that niggah with that big ol' monster dick. I know they had to pay you good for that!" Rhonda said, letting Tyneil know that she'd seen some of her movies. Then she went inside the gas station to pay and get her something to drink.

Now this is where shit got crazy. I'd finally got placed in a holding cell with a workin' phone, so I called my BM collect. Since she didn't have an account set up on her phone, our call was limited to a one-time complimentary 30-second call. In those few seconds I told her that the police really didn't have much on me, so they were just tryna make me sweat in hopes that I tell on myself. Rhonda assured me that everything was good with them and told me that they had just come from getting Lexi's things from the hotel. By that time, the time was up and she was transferred to where she needed to be to set up a call account.

Outside at my truck, Lexi was still on the phone with her mother, and Tyneil was taking selfies for her fans on IG. She was crouched down beside one of my rims when she noticed a nice baby blue Lexus coupé whip into the gas station. Tyneil had a thing for men with expensive costume cars, so she kept her eye on it as it pulled up beside Lexi and stopped. My sister had just ended her call when she noticed Tyneil's wide-eyed shocked expression just befo' she felt an arm wrap around her waist.

"Bitch, what! You thought you was just gonna leave me!" King Tivon barked in her ear as she screamed.

"Muthafucka, let her go!" Tyneil shouted as she ran over and immediately commenced to swinging her small fist at King Tivon's head and back.

"Von, please stop!" Alexis exclaimed while struggling to break free of his hold.

"Bitch, get the fuck off back!" he shouted at the same time as he punched Tyneil hard in her forehead, sending her wild swinging ass crashing to the ground, dazed. With her out of the way, he dragged Lexi who had suddenly became paralyzed with fear after seeing how hard he'd hit her cousin. "You coming home with me where you can get yo' fuckin' mind right."

Rhonda had just finished setting up the phone account when she walked outta the gas station and saw Alexis and Tyneil tussling and fighting with King Tivon. She immediately drew her gun and ran over to them.

"No, she ain't goin' no muthafuckin where with you!" my BM said, standing between them and the car with her gun pointed toward the ground in the direction of King Tivon. "Let her go. Now!"

"This don't got shit to do with you, bitch, so get the fuck outta my way."

"Or what? Man, I don't wanna shoot you!" Rhonda said as her gun wavered from her trying to decide if she wanted to risk hitting sis by tryna shoot him in the leg.

"Move!" he barked, taking a few steps closer toward Rhonda while using Lexi for a shield and forcing her to move with him. Rhonda stood her ground, tryna formulate a plan to get sis away from the crazy ass niggah without hurtin' her or having to kill him. All of a sudden King Tivon shoved my sister into Rhonda, then lunged at her simultaneously, grabbing her gun hand. Rhonda gasped in surprise, but didn't freeze up. She went right at him, slammin' her heavy fists into his face. She fought fiercely not to let him get ahold of her gun.

Alexis quickly recovered from being shoved to the ground and jumped on King Tivon's back just as he slammed Rhonda onto the hood of the Lexus. King Tivon slammed his elbow back, knocking my sister off of him, then he slammed Rhonda's wrist on the car hood so hard that she lost grip of the gun.

When the gun flew from her hand and hit the ground, Rhonda kicked it away from them so he couldn't get it and continued to fight. Tyneil quickly scooped the weapon up and staggered to her feet. She'd never used a gun before but she knew she would have to do somethin' to stop the crazy man. She ran over to the three tussling on the hood of the car and slapped King Tvon in the back of the head with the gun as hard as she could, then jumped back.

"Get the fuck off of 'em, muthafucka!" she shouted, aiming the gun. "Get on the ground!" she added when Rhonda landed a hard knee to his balls.

Rhonda took the gun from Tyneil's shaking hands. She was just in time because the police were pulling onto the gas station lot, answering the call of the clerk and the many witnesses who'd called 9-1-1.

"Tyneil, are you alright?" Rhonda asked, noticing the big knot beginning to swell on her forehead.

"Yeah, yeah. I'm okay!" she replied, shaking and tearing up from the adrenaline rushin' through her.

The three of 'em all went and sat in my truck while the police took their statements 'bout what happened. Sis made eye contact with King Tivon who was handcuffed and locked in back of a squad car. Then flipped him the finger as he was being hauled away.

Chapter 7

I think it had to have been, like, twelve hours after I'd spoken to my BM, that the detectives cut me loose. Like I said, they were only tryna make me sweat. They didn't have video of me from that night showing me with the gun or what actually happened. What they had from the camera only showed me buying drinks for Rhonda and her friends. The camera outside the club only showed me coming into the place and leaving, that's it, that's all. I'm guessing the witnesses who provided them with the information to find me were refusing to do anything more, because I was not put in a lineup. For me to be charged with anything at that point I would have to tell on myself and I wasn't talkin' loosely. Man, you know the rules, when they got you in cuffs, are to stay calm, give 'em your name then ask for a lawyer and then shut the hell up until they let you go or a lawyer comes to talk to you.

Well, I was being escorted to release staging when I looked over and spotted King Tivon's battered face. He was in the Booking area being fingerprinted. I wondered what happened to 'im because the blood on his clothes was fresh, and the damage to his face was way more than I remembered doing. He looked up and noticed me, standing in the release line. I smiled at him then gave him a double finger salute just as the deputy ordered for me to follow him out.

As soon as I was outside, I got to walkin' towards 6th Street, tryna put some distance between me and the jail fast.

I perambulated to my uncle Curt's crib in the Hillside Housing Projects. He wasn't home but this cute lil' chubbyish chick that lived next door to him let me use her phone to call him. Knowin' the chick likes me, I thought it was best not to call my BM from her phone.

Like I said, ol' girl was cute. She had a lil' baby weight on her from spittin' out five kids back-to-back. They were all young adults and all like a year apart. She was older than me, maybe the age I am now. At that time, I was in my early 30's. If you're familiar with the soul singer Jill Scott, that's who Georgia put you in the mind of kinda, sorta. Georgia would be Jill Scott on her worse day, put it like that. Don't get me wrong, I think Jill Scott is sexy as hell. Georgia was home alone drinking, as usual. Whenever I'd seen her in the past, she always had alcohol of some kind in her hand. She invited me inside to wait when it started to rain. I accepted her flirtatious invite and followed her juicy ass on inside her apartment. She was wearing skin-tight leggings and a black T-shirt that sat on top of her plump ass. The shirt had large shiny lips on the front of it with the words "Cum -N- Side" written beneath them.

"What you snickering about?" she asked when she heard me laugh at her shirt.

"I just read yo' shirt," I admitted, still smiling.

"I don't know what's so funny, unless you're scared to let me taste that dick?"

I should've known that she had somethin' on her freaky ass mind because of the way she kept mentioning that she was home alone. I said fuck it and went in. If she wanted some of this I got, why not give her a sample?

"Nah, I ain't scared. But why play with the lil' time we got? Why don't you come up outta them clothes and bend that ass over so I can give you what you really want?" I watched her face blush before she downed the rest of the cheap vodka in her glass and peeled herself right on outta them leggings. She wasn't shy, nor was she wearing panties, which I'd figured from the way her ass jiggled when she walked. Georgia tossed me a condom and I didn't waste no time doing no kinky shit or lookin' for a bedroom. I promptly spun her short thick self around and bent her over the arm of her sofa. I pounded her out for a good five minutes straight. In that time, she came at least twice. When I was about to bust, she spun back around, snatched off the condom and took me in her mouth. I followed the instructions on her shirt.

Afterwards, I cleaned up and I promised her that we would get together on a later date for more than a sample. Just the thought sent a shiver through her freaky self. I can't lie, she had a good shot. I understand why her late husband had put all them babies in her like he did. What I didn't understand was why was she single.

My uncle finally came and took me home. I lived downstairs from my mother mostly. I say mostly 'cause I'm always on the move and almost never there. My mother had her basement completely remodeled into an apartment. It has two nice size bedrooms; the master bedroom has an artificial electric fireplace, and the other has a full size hideaway bed that folds out of the wall. They both have walk-in closets. The stainless steel kitchen has an island with an electric range stove and subzero refrigerator, a breakfast bar sitting just off a small dining room, a large living room, and a split bathroom with a standalone granite and glass walk-in shower. I did my thang with its furnishing, straight up. If you see it, you'd never believe that it was a basement nor that it's located smack dead in the middle of the ghetto.

I'd texted Rhonda from my uncle's phone and told her I was out and heading home to get cleaned up. She replied, informing me that she had been called in to work and that my truck and everything was at her house. She also told me that my sister was with Tyneil. After showering, I dressed in black Dickie cargo pants, T-shirt and black Nike Air Max 90s. I grabbed my prepaid burner phone and then walked the

4½ city blocks between my place and Rhonda's. Once there, I spent a little time with the kids, who'd obviously fallen in love with their new auntie Lexi. That's what they call her, "New Auntie Lexi".

After I dropped off the junk food that my babies had talked me into walkin' down to the corner store and buying for 'em, I got the keys to my truck and left them nice an' sugared up for their grandmother to deal with. Inside my truck I found my two cell phones, wallet, and gun where I'd left 'em. I never had a doubt that it wouldn't be. My BM is just that good of a woman. That's why she's the HBIC in my life.

Dawg, man, if it was up to me I would've married her a long time ago. But though she wouldn't admit it, Rhonda was scared of that type of commitment. She says that she wants me to be done with the streets before she says yes to becoming Mrs. Assa Reigns. So being the true thug that I am, I foolishly chose to keep having my cake and eating it too, as they say.

Before heading over to kick it with my sister, I once again went out to my storage unit and swopped the Yukon for the Camaro. I wasn't on no stuntin' shit or nothin'. It's just that the Yukon was too tall to fit in my garage at home and I didn't like to park it on the street longer than I had to, but I didn't stay in the Camaro neither. I went home and swopped it out for my black and chrome two-door Chevy Tahoe. I drove it the most out of all of my vehicles because I love the hard bass from its 15,000-watt stereo system. I remember this time when my lil' brother had locked his girl in the backseat then gradually cranked the volume up on her. The bass from her favorite song, *Bottoms Up*, by Trey Songs, had her crying and hyperventilating. That shit there was funny. It was mean of him, but still funny.

At Tyneil's West side condominium I sat and got the play-by-play rundown of the situation that took place between them and King Tivon at the gas station.

"That mess was insane!" I said when they were about done with the story. "I seen 'im when I was gettin' released. I wondered who had fucked him up again."

"Yeah, his punk ass would've been a dead dog if yo' girl hadn't have taken the gun from me," Tyneil said, "You see what bitch did to my face?"

I did, hell, you couldn't help but notice the big ass knot on her discolored forehead on her light, bright, damn near white face. Seeing her pretty self all bruised up made me wish I'd really beat King Tivon's ass. My sister didn't look all that bad. All she really had wrong with her was a tiny cut on her bottom lip. I wanted to know what my BM looked like after the scuffle. Rhonda's was creamy milk chocolate complexion, almost as dark as me, so it would take a lot for bruises to show on her. For her to be at work at the time, I guessed she didn't look too bad. But like me, when that money calls, she's gonna go get it.

Speakin' of money calling. I had received a few calls from my guys saying they needed me to ride down on them, and a text from Lil Dave and Chese sayin' that they were 'bout out as well. Knowing that Lexi was flying back home the following day at noon, I asked her did she wanna ride with me.

"Y'all two go ahead. I'm not goin' no place I don't have to looking like this!" Tyneil replied as she posted pics of her battered face on her social media pages. People are just strange like that. Every time I see or hear someone say that they don't wanna be seen or they don't wanna deal with others then turn right around and post pics and comments on social media, it makes me wonder what's the disconnect in their heads when it comes to the real world and social media. Tyneil had to know that way more people were going to see her all fucked up on there than if she went out with us, especially as famous as she is. I couldn't do nothin' but shake my head. "AR, are you spending the night over here with us?

I'd feel so much better with you here in me," she said with a devious smile.

"You do know we're somethin' like cousins, right?"

"Something like cousins isn't the same as we are. You can help me make a movie and we can call it Kissing Cousins." Lexi and I had to laugh with her when she said that.

"Ty, you crazy. I'll see you when I get back," sis told her, pulling me out of the door. "Damn, big brother, how many cars do you have?" she inquired as we approached the Tahoe.

"A bunch. I love cars. It's what I do for a living beside hustle in these streets day in and day out. I buy, sell and repair cars. It's always that one car of truck that I just can't seem to part with right away once I'm done fixing it up though!" I explained.

After gathering the wurk I needed, sis surprised me by helping me cook, weigh and package up what I needed for my hard sales. Alexis explained that her knowledge of how to do it came from the love of her life who was a dope boy, so she learned everything from him. When I asked what happened to him, she emotionally explained his love for fast cars and how he'd lost control of his car during a race and crashed into a wall at over a 120 mph, instantly killing himself. I dried her tears and gave her the hug that I should've been there to give her the day it happened.

Chapter 8

Moving this sob story along. I did end up spending the night over Tyneil's with my sister. I was sitting on the couch reading and replying to Facebook posts when Tyneil emerged from her bedroom only wearing a pink T-shirt that stopped just at her wide hips. Her hair was pulled back in a loose ponytail and she didn't have on any make-up.

"Wha'cha doing?" she asked me as she sat down beside me.

"Nothin, just chillin'," I answered, and the next thing I know: she'd my monster outta my pants, stroking it with both of her soft hands around it. "Ty—"

"Shhh!" she cut me off, staring in my eyes while still slowly stroking my length so it stood nice and strong. Tyneil cupped the tip of my hardness. "I need to know if it tastes as good as it feels in my hands," she uttered under her breath.

I gave in and guided her head down into my lap until my tip was pressed against her soft pouty lips. With a quick flicker of her tongue she opened her mouth as wide as she could to fit it in and was only able to get maybe three inches in. That was about all that would fit before I felt her throat. The excitement of having her lips wrapped around my shaft had me excited. After a few moments, Tyneil pulled her mouth off my hardness and stood up. With one quick motion I stripped her shirt off, then snatched her panties off. She moaned as she climbed on top of me so she could control things to ensure that she got what she wanted better.

Grabbing hold of my length, she guided it to her swollen warmth and slowly lowered herself down in it. I put my hands on her waist and started lifting her up and down, trying to push farther inside her with every stroke. She gently built up to a tempo that was so good to her. All I could do was throw back my head and close my eyes and enjoy the pleasure. I finally gave her one hard thrust and held her there. Tyneil sat still for a few hot seconds soaking me with her wetness before suddenly kissing me, then began pumping up and down on me. I could feel my climax building. As she cried out in pleasure, I pulled her down hard onto my lap and she came. As soon as she came down from her orgasm, she jumped off of me, dropped to her knees and took my hardness in her mouth so she could find out how good my release tasted.

Just as I was about to bust, I woke up. It was just a dream. I was still fully dressed on the couch where I'd fallen asleep alone. I can't lie to you though, waking up and seeing Tyneil thick fine ass sashaying around in only a flesh colored bra and panties did make my swollen joint throb for release. I kinda questioned, *are we really considered cousins*? Yeah, I'd seen her naked and gettin' crammed and sucked in her movies. That's where my dream came from, but having her half-naked in front of me was somethin' different.

Anyways, while we were saying our goodbyes to my sister at the airport, King Tivon was being bailed outta jail. Because he don't live in Wisconsin, he was allowed to return to his home on the West coast but ordered to surrender his passport and not to have contact with Alexis. He assured them that he would comply with the conditions of his bond release since KT and sis don't live together, well, not officially anyway. They just kinda floated between his place and hers. Each of 'em having their own key and keepin' a few personal items at each other's cribs.

The first two things that sis did when she got home was go clear all of her things out of KT's place with the help of her lil' sisters, and then changed the locks on her front door. For like two weeks, things were cool. KT, surprisingly, didn't once in that time call, text, or come over to her crib. But then all of a sudden, he flipped the script. At first, he would show up at the clubs where she would be working, always getting the VIP section closest to her and sitting so he could keep her in his line of sight at all times during her sets. That started happening more and more. Because of KT's fame, the clubs that Alexis DJ for didn't dare deny him entry. Sis came up with the idea to start dating with the encouragement of Rhonda who she kept in contact with more than she did me, it seemed.

Alexis knew this bouncer that had a liking for her. He wasn't bad lookin' or nothin'. He was tall, light brown-skinned and very well-built. His intimidating size was all sis was after. She wanted to be seen with someone who she thought would make KT think twice about fuckin' with her again. But seeing them together only kicked up King Tivon's jealousy. Not more than a month into Lexi's new relationship with the big Bouncer, KT had his Crip gang buddies to corner and beat the man within inches of his life and give him a strict warning that they would kill him the next time they see him anywhere near Lexi. So I don't have to tell you that that was the end of their relationship.

Even though sis had no proof that KT was behind her boyfriend's assault and sudden breakup with her, she knew in her heart that it was his doing. The incident was enough for her to send the police to King Tivon's place to remind him of the conditions of his release. After their visit, things calmed down again. He stopped poppin' up at the places where she was working and stopped posting up outside of the clubs at the end of the night watching her pack her equipment into her Trailblazer. Everything just stopped. Knowing him, that made sis curious, so she made up fake social media pages to help her keep track of his movements. She found that he'd been spending a lot of time in California and Chicago doing his music. Having the social media setup put her mind at ease. Mine and Rhonda's too.

Chapter 9

The peace that my sister had came to a crashin' end that changed our lives. It happened one night after she'd spent some time out with friends and family celebrating her lil' sister's 21st birthday. Alexis is the oldest of her mother's children, I'm the oldest of our father's children. Her mother has always loved me like one of her own, and Alexis's younger siblings love the fact that they now had me to put up against sis when she got on 'em about things.

Well, anyways, Lexi was a lil' tipsy when she made it home after the party. Knowing that she was there alone, she started stripping off her clothes as soon as she walked through the door. She staggered through the house, leaving items of clothing wherever they fell. By the time she made it to her bathroom to turn on the shower, get the smell of alcohol and the birthday girl's vomit off of her, she was only dressed in her Victoria's Secrets. In the bathroom Lexi set the water temperature for her shower, then hung her bra on a hook on the back of the bathroom door and headed into her bedroom. At the same time, as she caught the aroma of weed smoke and Usher Cologne, she sensed a presence behind her in the dark. Before she could turn to fight, King Tivon's hand was locked tightly around her throat, cutting off her ability to scream and breathe easily. He instantaneously wrapped his other had around her body, pinning both of her arms to her sides.

"Bitch, why in the fuck is you comin' in this late? What the fuck!" he shouted. Sis could smell alcohol and weed on his breath. "Who were you out with? Huh, who?"

"Let me go! I wasn't with no fuckin' body!" she managed to respond. She hated herself for whimpering and for being in his total control. So she got mad and tried to fight to break free of his hold. She thrashed from side to side wildly. When that didn't work, she stomped down on his foot as hard as she could with her bare feet.

As soon as he let go of her throat, he rapidly slammed his fist into the back of her head several times, knocking the fight right outta her. Stunned from the hard blows to the head, Lexi found herself being shoved face down on her bed and her panties being ripped off of her then stuffed in her mouth as a gag. Lying face down on the bed with her arms pinned above her head and King Tivon's crushing weight on top of her, she whimpered as she prepared herself to be raped by a man she had once loved. Just before the pain commenced, she told herself if she didn't fight him and just lay there he wouldn't hurt her. Nausea from pain and fear caused Alexis to pass out.

Later, when she came to, she found that she was in the bed alone. The house was quiet, which she knew was wrong because she remembered turning on the shower. Which meant her rapist ex-boyfriend had turned it off. She sat up stung and hurting all over. She didn't want to move but at the same time she felt extra dirty, so she began moving towards the bathroom to get herself cleaned up. She spotted that KT had left her back door slightly ajar, lettin' her know how he'd gotten inside. She ran over and slammed it close, then locked it. Just to be safe, she jammed a kitchen chair against the doorknob.

Alexis didn't bother checkin' her place; she knew after what he'd done to her, that he was long gone. She went in the bathroom, turned back on the hot shower and climbed beneath the spray of water. She scrubbed herself until it hurt, then just sat in the tub with the shower still spraying down on her. Lil' sis sat like that until she felt the hot water turn cold. By that time, she was all cried out. She knew that she wasn't safe in that house, so she dressed then went to work, packing. By the time she was done, it was dark outside again.

My phone call startled her and she almost didn't answer for me. She felt too humiliated to talk to anyone, but she answered for me.

"Wudd it do, sis!" I greeted, happy to get her on the phone.

"AR—AR, he, he—hurt me," she stammered, sobbing again.

"What! Is he there now?"

"No."

"I'm on my way. I'm finna jump on the next plane—"

"No, don't!" she exclaimed. "I don't want you gettin' in any trouble. I'm alright. I'm okay."

"You may be but I'm not," I replied, not being convinced by the sound of her voice, "Lexi, I'ma come there and make sure you're safe. I have to or I'ma go crazy. It would be reckless for me to up and leave what I'm in the middle of right this moment, but know that I'm on my way. Until I get there I want you to go stay over yo' mama house or someplace where you're not alone. Do you hear me?"

"Yes, big brother. I love you!"

"I love you."

"Bro, let me get off this phone so I can finish packing and get outta here like you told me to."

With that said, I let her off the phone. Man, I was heated. The only thing on my mind was finding the niggah and puttin' him in the hospital or the grave. As soon as I was done bustin' my move down in Chicago with my connect for 3½ bricks, I was going to get on the next thing smokin' to Seattle. When I got off of the phone with Lexi, I called my BM and told her that the niggah had jumped on my sister again, because all Alexis had told me was that KT had hurt her—

not that he'd in fact raped her. Had she told me that, I would've jumped on an airplane right from Chicago and left my partner to deal with the plug on his own. Rhonda told me that she was going to call her and find out how bad things were because she knew that she could get more outta her than I could, as mad as I was.

After promising to be careful, I got off the phone with her. I still had to wait almost another two hours down in the Windy for my plug to show up. When he finally did show, he didn't have all of what we needed, so we had to wait another hour for his guy to bring us another brick. For our trouble he tossed us another 1½ on a front. And just like that I wasn't mad anymore; well, I wasn't hot with him anymore.

By 9:00 p.m. Lexi was crossing state lines on her way to the only place that she felt that she'd be kept safe from the crazy man. She stormed her poor Trailblazer through state after state on the phone with either her mother, one of her sisters, Tyneil or Rhonda the whole way. Sis told my BM not to tell me that she was on her way there to stay 'cause she wanted it to be a surprise. So when I made it back to *Kilwaukee*, I went straight over my BM's house because I wanted to talk to her face-to-face about my sister. When we walked in, I found her in her bedroom as usual watching something on her laptop. Being nosey, I looked to see what she was watching and saw Tyneil on the screen dressed as a dominatrix in a shiny black leather outfit, complete with a long blonde wig and thigh-high boots. She was sucking off a tall slim black dude. I glanced back at my BM and saw that she was spellbound by the way Tyneil was taking on his huge length. The guy on the screen slid between a redhead girl's legs and started to fuck her hard and fast while Tyneil whacked him on the ass with a wooden paddle.

My joint was instantly hard as hell, as it is almost always when I have Rhonda's sexy self to myself. Knowing that she was turned on by what she was watching, I pulled my hardness out, and put it in her hand. She began to stroke it slowly, without taking her eyes off the computer screen. After a minute, she repositioned herself so that she was kneeling on the bed and started helping me outta my clothes, feverishly sucking my neck while I fondled her hard nipples and big soft titties. When I was undressed, she made her way down my body and started sucking my dick insatiably.

As her head bobbed in my lap, I looked over and saw that the guy on the TV was now ass-fucking a different girl with two-tone blue and hot pink hair. I spun Rhonda around, pulled her nightie up over her plump ass, and her panties aside, and shoved my hardness all of the way inside her. When I began pounding her out, she moaned, cumming all over my length, as she urged me to pound her harder and faster. I did as instructed, and in no time I felt her whole body began convulsing. When I couldn't take any more of her good good, I let go, and released buried deep in her.

Rhonda turned around and took my dick in her throat. I let her have her fun, then I traded places on the bed with her, pulling her over my face, putting my tongue to work until she came again and again.

Afterwards, as we lay, we talked about what I'd come over to talk about. My BM convinced me not to go to Seattle until I heard from my sister again. She also said that I should give her some time to get her thoughts together. I agreed to do that. After I caught my breath, I cleaned up, dressed, and dived into doing what I do in the streets. As long as I kept busy, Alexis will have all of the time she needed.

Chapter 10

When me and RG made it back to Milwaukee, we had a bunch of sales waiting on us. By myself I had a little over a brick and a quarter in hard, gone as soon as I got in the kitchen and put it together, and another 6 ounces soft—gone as soon as I got it weighed out. Man, if it wasn't for the plug throwin' in that extra, I would've had to hit the highway first thing in the morning to re-up again. With the extra work, I knew I could sleep in until around noon. You know I'm not one of them fools that turn their phones off at a certain time so they can go fuck off at the club or with a broad. I wasn't tryna be out sellin' dope fo'ever. So many hustlers out there in the streets play the game like it's a game, when that far from the truth. You can't be halfway in the streets. There's no such thing. You're either all the way in or all of the way out. Dawg, I've heard so many smart fools say that they only hustle sometimes. They don't understand that it only takes one time to get you a lifetime behind these bars. I can almost use myself as an example of that. Even though I was doing my thang, I hated being in the streets, and I had an end game that I was workin' towards.

My bad, sometimes I just gotta vent on some shit. But anyways, after I made my rounds through the city, I hit the highway and headed up North. I met up with Chese and Lil Dave at a truck stop to give them each the wurk they needed. Lil Dave don't usually fuck with coke but his father-in-law had asked him could he get him an ounce half-hard, half-soft to take with him on his hunting trip with his buddies. I don't know why he just didn't get it from lil' cuz but it was mo' bread in my pocket, so I didn't question him. They wanted me to come on up to Appleton and kick it with them but I really wasn't in the mood with my mind on that fuck-boy puttin' his hands on my lil' sister again, so I passed with a promise to hook up with them after the weekend rush.

 I turned down kickin' it with lil' cuz 'nem, only for my uncle Curt call me over to the lil' get-together that he was throwing at his crib. Since I'd made all of my rounds for the time being, I didn't have anything to do at the time. I couldn't afford to shut off my phone because of the weekend rush, so kickin' it with my kids was out. I always shut everything down when I'm with them, because nothin' else matters to me but seeing my babies smile and enjoying their time out with me. And I couldn't afford to miss no money, because a used car lot had recently gone up for sale and I wanted it. With the car lot I'd be set right where I wanted to be, which is to be no longer pitching bricks at the prisons.

 The party at uncle Curt's was jumpin' as always when my family get together like this. His parties be mostly family, so it really don't be no bullshit like when you go out to the clubs. I had to make a run to serve one of the guys a few balls. He needed 3 hard and 1 soft. I don't understand why he don't just spend the bread to get himself all the way right instead of being taxed constantly buying the lil' wurk the way he does, but that's him. I'ma only offer a niggah an easier way once and if he don't got mind enough to jump on my offer, then fuck 'im! It's just mo' cash in my bank. I returned to the party $500 richer, and ran into Georgia who was lookin' fine as hell that night. I'd never seen her really dressed up before. She had her hair done instead of having it in the ponytail that I'm used to seeing it in. Her make-up made her look way younger, and the firm-fitting short cream colored dress that she had on made her titties sit-up just right, and the way the dress flared out at the bottom made her sexy legs look way longer than they actually are on her 5'1" inch frame. The drink in her hand was the only thing that remained the same about her.

"Damn, gurl, who you out here lookin' all sexy for? I think I might be jealous!" I joked, complimenting her at the same time when she walked out to me.

"Don't be. I got dressed up for you."

"Whuteva! Tell a niggah anything," he said sarcastically.

"I'm serious, I wanted you to see me when I put on some clothes. I asked Curt to call you over here since you didn't leave me your number that day."

"My bad, it wasn't done on purpose," I apologized, shaking my head, feelin' a tiny bit shame about my negligence.

"It's okay. I know your mind was elsewhere. Shit, so was mine." She giggled and blushed at her memory of us.

"So you wanted me to see you in clothes that makes me wanna take you outta them?" I said, running my eyes lustfully over her body.

"Well, if that's what you want, my house is empty. You promised me a full ride when you had more time and you being here at this party tells me that have some time on your hands. Unless you were just talkin'?"

"Nawl, I wasn't just talkin'. I kinda do and don't gotta lot of time on my hands right now."

"What does that mean?" she inquired, looking up into my eyes with her hand on her hip.

"I'm actually working right now, so when my phone rings I gotta go. I can always come back after I handle my business, but I gotta go when it rings. If you don't have an issue with that," I closed the distance between us and discreetly slid my hands up her thighs and palmed her ass beneath her dress. "Then lead the way so I can pay what I owe."

"Umm, I understand." She agreed, blushing and smiling as she took my hand and towed me back over to her place.

Just like before, her place was cool, clean and quiet. I knew the only one of her kids that live there with her was her eighteen-year-old son who spent most of his time with his guys out chasin' girls like a young man was supposed to do. "Give me a minute please. I don't wanna mess up this dress because if you end up having to leave soon I'm going back to the party because I know you're not coming back."

"Go do what you do. But aye, if I say it I mean it. Know that!" I told her as she walked into the bathroom. A short time later, she came out wearing this sexy silk camisole and her heels. "Damn, you really did have this all planned out, didn't you?"

"I'm trying to show you how much I'll do for my man."

"So that's what this is about, you're tryna lock me down, make me yo' man and all that?"

"I'm not trying lock nobody down who don't wanna be. For me you became my man when you fucked me the way you did."

Now I should've known better than to fuck her again after she told me that, but at the time I wasn't tryna read off into all that. I was just eager to experience what she had planned for me. I ogled her as she picked up a remote control and tapped a button that filled the room with soft music. Then she sashayed over to me, kissed the corner of my mouth and pulled my shirt off over my head. A lusty moan escaped her lips as she dragged her hands down my body. I cuffed her ass and gave her the kiss that she really wanted. I felt the shiver of need that shot down her body. Georgia broke our kiss and needingly began sucking my neck down to my chest, she licked my nipples at the same time as she was pushin' both my pants and underwear down my legs. She took my semi-hardness into her warm mouth just as I'd finished stepping out of my clothes and shoes.

I let her enjoy suckin' me because it was clearly something she specialized in from the way she repeatedly teased my tip with her lips and tongue. Each suggestive gesture she made promised me something more sensual. I was so hard that when she took my full length in her mouth and started sucking, I came almost instantly; she swallowed, then continued sucking. When I was nice and hard again, I stood her up, stripped her out of the camisole, then lifted her up off her feet and sucked one of her hard nipples in my mouth as I carried her over to the foot of the bed. Georgia had locked her legs tightly around my waist. I guess she was afraid I'd drop her, or maybe I was the first man to ever pick her up like that. I don't know, but I laid her down on the bed and she ordered me to fuck her.

So, I rubbed my hardness between her neatly shaved blossom's lips before pushing slightly inside her. She was so hot and wet it seemed like she had come as I stuck the tip of my length straight inside her. It was hard for me not to push all of the way inside her wetness. The way I was teasingly fuckin' her with only the head was driving her crazy. When I finally did slam it all the way in, Georgia screamed and clawed my shoulders. That's when I flipped her over, pulled her on her knees so that she was face down, ass up, and I went to work. I fucked her so hard that she was cumming like a running river and speaking gibberish. Tired and covered in sweat, I traded places with her, pullin' her on top and immediately pushin' my throbbing hardness back in her. She didn't play with it; she went to work, bouncing and rocking us to a breathtaking climax.

Chapter 11

Surprisingly, my phones hadn't rung once during our lil' fuck fest, so I just enjoyed the lil' down time by layin' there with Georgia's head on my chest and her legs entangled around mine. Our few moments of silence came to an end when Georgia started talkin'. I'm not into all that pillow talkin' stuff. I don't know why women think after sex is the best time to talk to me. I'ma feed-me-and-bleed-me guy. If a woman can cook, she can get a lot more outta me than she could with my dick down her throat. But I answered a few of her questions as honestly as I could. Yes, I told her about my BM and kids and made sure that she knew that they were always priority in my life even though I was more or less single. What got my attention most in our conversation was when she got to tellin' me about herself. Georgia explained that the reason she was single is that the men she'd had in her life after her divorce all seemed to want to beat on her and take advantage of her because she was generous with her money. She told me about her job working as a pharmacist assistant and a part-time home health care aid.

"Why do you still live in Hillside? I mean, it's not like you can't afford to buy you a crib somewhere decent."

"I do own a house. It's a duplex on 55th and Burleigh that my two oldest live in. I stay here because all my friends are here and it's close to my jobs and downtown!" she explained. Like I knew it would sooner or later happen, my phones started sounding off. "Damn, just when I was about to try and get another round outta you," she half pouted.

"If I can come back over tonight I will, but if not I'll be here so we can do it all again tomorrow night," I told her, collecting my things and goin' into the bathroom to get cleaned up, redressed, and to reply to the texted orders that were flooding in.

Georgia walked me to the door and thanked me like I was a delivery guy or something. I could see the appreciation as well as the loneliness in her light brown eyes. I gave her a hug and told her I'll get up with her later. Then I went and made a quick $2,700. By then it was too late for me to go back over Georgia's crib, so I texted her and told her not to wait up and I'll see her later. Then I took my ass home. Once there, I took a quick shower and went to sleep. Well, I tried to go to sleep but two more calls came in. The only thing good was that both callers were allowed to come by my crib. The first was my cousin—Blacc—who needed both some wurk and cash because he'd got hit at the casino. I didn't have no problem with giving him anything because he always kept it straight with me. Plus, when he gambles he seems to win more than he loses; either way, he was good for whuteva. The second was my fellow thug—Tank—who really didn't want nothin' but some of my slut smoke. Slut smoke is what he calls the weed I kept. He said he calls it that 'cause I don't smoke and I was always with a female who does. He paid me the lil' cash he owed me on some wurk I'd given him a couple of flips ago and got some weed for him and his van full of hoes.

Tank was trying his hand at pimpin'. I can't lie he was comin' up fast. He started with two hoes to begin with but now he was up to six in a little over a month. He had some walkin' the tracks and others workin' in strip clubs. I made sure to remind him that our goal is to get money and put it to good use so we could leave the streets alone. I didn't have to but I did anyway and I told him that. Hoe money was slow money and dope money is fo' sho money.

When Tank left, I took my ass to bed but as soon as I closed my eyes good, Rhonda was ringing my phone. "Hello!" I quickly answered the call because she never really calls me that early unless somethin' was wrong. And since I knew she didn't have to work the night before, I thought something bad had happened.

What it was was that my sister had come back to Milwaukee and had driven straight to Rhonda's house just the way they'd planned it out. What wasn't a part of the plan was Alexis breakin' down cryin' in Rhonda arms and confessing that she'd been sexually assaulted by King Tivon. My BM gave her something to help her relax, then let her cry herself to sleep. Rhonda called me over to the house so I could be there when Alexis woke up.

Chapter 12

Back over in Seattle, King Tivon was going through it mentally. He was drinkin', mumbling to himself and pacing and forth in his condo. KT knew he'd fucked up when he did what he'd done to my sister. He spent all of the day gettin' high as clouds, drinkin, smokin', snortin' and all that. If it was there he was doing it, he couldn't even remember driving over to Lexi's house. The fool was paranoid because of what he'd done to my sister and 'cause he didn't know if she was alive or not. KT was so mentally and emotionally gone that his mind only gave him flashes of the memory of what happened, so all he knew was that Lexi wasn't movin' when he left her. He'd tried calling her several times with no answer. He thought about going over to check on her, but then if she was dead he knew that he was the police number one suspect. KT needed to come up with a plausible alibi just in case the police came knockin'.

His hollow concern for my sister had turned into rage by the next time he tried callin' her. This time, instead of being sent to voicemail, he was told that the number was no longer in service. That told him that sis had changed her phone number on his fool ass.

"How could she change her fuckin' number on me? Why in the hell is she still trippin' over that lil' shit?" he questioned himself out loud as he started pacing again. "I fuck up one time, one time I check her in public and she ain't tryna fuck with me no more. She wouldn't be trippin' if it wasn't for her bitch ass brother. If the niggah really is her brother . . . why won't she let me apologize and make it up to her? She should be good after the way I fucked her. I fucked her to sleep." He grinned at the false memory. The ringing of his phone snapped him briefly outta his head. "Yeah?"

"Gang gang, Wuddup! You good?" the voice asked, a bit concerned after having earlier seen the front end damage done to his friend's Range Rover.

"Not really, no."

"I'm askin' 'cause I see you done smacked up the Range. What happen with that?"

"All I did was love that bitch an' she don't appreciate shit," King Tivon mumbled.

"Whud you say KT? You mumbling an' shit, I couldn't hear you." When he didn't respond, his friend said, "Say, Cuz, I'm thinkin' you ain't in yo' right mind right now so check it, I'ma go grab a bottle and bend back on you."

KT wasn't listenin' but he knew that he didn't want to be bothered with nobody. He told his guy that he was good, then ended the call before he could protest. "Where in the hell is she? Probably at her mother's. That's where she usually goes when we get into it and she needs to cool off. I need to go over there and make her talk to me. I can make her hear me out." He continued to mumble to himself, grabbing his keys and rushin' out the door. On the way outta the parking garage he spotted a police car parked out in front of his building. Seeing the car just sittin' there kicked back up his paranoia; that's when he came up with a plan of escape. King Tivon drove outta the garage and parked facing the opposite direction of the squad car. Then, keepin' his eyes on the squad, he called the police and reported his Range Rover stolen. After giving 9-1-1 all of the info they needed, he got outta the truck, marched up to the officer seated in the squad car watchin' him, and shot him three times then ran and jumped back in his truck and sped away. In his escape from the scene he sideswiped a mail delivery truck as he turned the corner.

"Fuck the police, I spray 'em down an' lay low underground. Keep a whole drumstick so when I spit it's lease a hundred rounds..." he rapped in a craze that he didn't know that he'd slipped into. When he reached a good place to stop, he gathered what he wanted out of the battered SUV, then set it on fire. About two blocks over he called an Uber all headed to the nearest car rental. From there he swung by Lexi's mother's house. When he got there he knew she was gone from the way she'd left the garage door open. "Where the fuck is she?" he asked himself, then decided to head down to California.

Dawg, man, when I say the niggah was trippin' outta his fuckin' mind, I mean it. The police officer that he'd murdered wasn't even thinkin' about 'im. He was just sittin' in the squad car waiting for his partner to return with the coffee he'd asked for. An' since the radio was quiet, the officer put on his dark sunglasses and closed his eyes for a quick nap. The first and last time he'd seen King Tivon is when he opened his eyes to see what was casting the shadow that blocked the warm sun and found a gun being pointed at him just befo' KT had shot him in the face. The crazy man had killed the officer for nothin' at all. And the crazy part about it all is that he had done it and made a clean getaway in broad daylight. That shid crazy, 'cause all I'd done was rough him up and all typa muthafuckas had called the police on me but that fool killed a whole police officer and nobody, not even the officer's partner, had seen anything.

Chapter 13

Fuck! I was so mad after sis explained what that punk had done to her. All I saw was red. Her voice had become a murmur. Without sayin' a word, I just got up and walked outta the house. I got in my Crown Vic and just started drivin' and thinkin'. I ended up down at the Lakefront where I parked and walked from one end of the beach to the other end. I calmed down and took peace that she was in the Mil where I could protect her.

A few days later, maybe more like a week, Alexis started talkin' about getting her own place. I tried to talk her into staying with me since I had an extra bedroom; plus, I was hardly ever at home. Sis wasn't going. She said she didn't want to accidentally bring someone to my place that I didn't want to know where I lay my head. Tyneil offered to let her stay with her too, but sis turned her down too sayin' that Tyneil had way too many visitors running in and out of her spot for her to be comfortable there. I really didn't want her living that far away from me no way, so I agreed with her on that.

My aunt and uncle own a bunch of houses and I remember my auntie telling me that the lady who used to rent her two-bedroom single family house over on 20th Street had up and moved out of state, leavin' pretty much all of her furniture behind. Since Alexis had just done the exact same thing, I felt like it would be prefect fo' her. My auntie—Amy—made me talk to my shit-talkin' ass uncle Ed about renting the place out to my sister. Unc talked his shit like I knew he would. In the end though, he agreed to it, because I'm the son that his saggy ass balls couldn't produce. I even got him to him to lower the rent for a few months until sis got settled in good. Unc still made me pay the rent up for three months up front. Alexis loved the place as soon as she saw it. She offered me my money back because she has a nice savings account, but I refused by telling her to hold on to it 'til I needed it. Man, that need came sooner than I thought it would.

The Feds came through and did their sweep of Milwaukee. You know after they do thang and collect all of the people that they'd built cases on, the streets dry up and the prices go up. RG, my partner in crime's plug down in Chicago had gotten caught up in the sweep, and *my* plug down there was MIA. So we were kinda forced to do our own thangs to stay afloat. Now, since RG only hustled in Milwaukee, I was in a better standing than him. Remember, I really don't fool around in the Mil; I hit the highways. Doing so, I was able to maximize my profits.

One day I was up in LaCrosse moving hundred dollar grams of hard and soft, when a bunch of my clientele started requesting pills, prescription pills, to be exact. Before then, I'd never really paid attention to the pill poppers, but when I opened my eyes I saw the money to be made and on my drive back home I know who to go to, to put me in the game. I called Georgia.

"Hey, you! I'm surprised to be hearing from you after the way you stood me up and had been blowing me off."

"Ma, I didn't mean to do none of that you takin', and I really don't wanna have this discussion over the phone," I said, knowing the venom in her voice was well deserved.

"Well, you know where I live at."

"Georgia, I'm tryna apologize. If you don't wanna fuck with me nomo' after you hear what I have to say, it'll be fucked up. But I'll respect it. I'm hoping we can still be friends when it's all said and done with."

"Friends? Niggah, I told you when you put that dick on me like you did, that you were my man. Now here you are coming at me with this friend shit. Fuck you, AR! You hurt me and you know you did. That's why you coming at me with this bullshit!" she snapped.

"First, bitch, stop yellin' at me! I heard you loud and clear when you said what you said. I know it was messed up but you need to give me a chance to explain. I'm not tryna sit up in yo' crib with you because all that's gonna end up happening is us fuckin' and can't no clear understanding be made when that happen. I'm not tryna pacify you or stand on you, but since you screaming that I'm yo' man, stop bein' a bitch and take yo' smart mouth ass in yo' room and put on somethin' sexy for me, so I can take you out to eat someplace nice. I'll be there to pick you up in about an hour!" I said then hung up on her to let her know I didn't want to hear nothing else from her.

When I pulled up, she was sittin' out on the porch with my aunt, Rene, talkin'. I didn't bother to get outta the car, but the way she jumped up and locked up her place told me that she didn't expect me too. I waved hi to my auntie, then had to shake my head at how good Georgia looked in the tight white jeans, gold silk blouse and matching gold high heels. It still fucks my head up how she always be sittin' on the porch dressed like a ragdoll, as pretty as she is.

"Is this good for you, babe, or do you want me to go change quick?" she inquired befo' she sat in the car.

"I'm not sure. I think I need you to do a slow turn for me so I can see how that ass lookin' in them jeans!" I said, making her smile.

"You can see all the ass you want if I decide to accept your apology," she replied, dropping down in the seat. "Babe, since this is my time, can we go get in your black sports car?"

"Sports car? You talkin' 'bout the Camaro?"

"Yeah, if that's the black and gold one?"

"Yeap, that's it. Why do you wanna get in that car? Let me guess, because you got on gold and you wanna match the car?" I said, already heading to swop out the Cadillac DeVille for the Camaro.

"Wrong. I got on white too, crazy, so I match this car too if that was it. I just want to ride in it. I always like cars shaped like that."

We talked about her interest in sports cars pretty much the whole way to the garage. I offered to let her drive but she didn't want to in her heels. I don't understand it and didn't ask why, so don't ask me. Your guess is as good as mine. So, I drove us to this nice lil' restaurant out by Brown Deer that served this jumbo lump crab cake dish that I like. Yeah, I could've just taken her to Red Lobster's and got something similar for way cheaper and her drunk ass would've it just the same. But I needed to butter her up and to show her how it feels to fuck with a boss.

By no plan of my own, the outfit I was wearing complemented hers well. I was dressed in a deep brown, tan and white cardigan, crisp white button-up, tan slacks and white Guess loafers. Right through the door the smiling maitre d' greeted us and seated us at a nice table for two. Georgia was all smiles.

"They have some good food here and crab cake dish that I like. Do you mind if I order it for the both of us? I believe it's served with a red wine."

"No, I don't mind. Whatever you wanna do. It's just nice to be treated nice and taken someplace new for a change!" she said, lookin' at me shyly. How many of your lil' girlfriends have you been here with?"

"None, because I don't date girls. As far as women that I do mess with, you would be the second I've been here with a few times though. I brung my mother here for her birthday and I've had a few business meetings out here."

"AR, you do know I know what you do, right?"

"I believe you think you know what I do, and that part that you do know I could use yo' help with. But I don't wanna talk about that right now."

"Okay, so then tell me why it took so long for me to hear from you or to see you."

"Even though I know Auntie Rene had more than likely told you about my sister already, I'ma tell you again so you can hear it straight from me," I said, then explained everything that went on with sis without much detail. That conversation moved right on to my issue with tryna find a good drug connect, and from there to her job. "How would you like to make some extra money?"

"I would love to make some extra money. It all depends on what all I have to do to get it?"

"You don't have to do anything that you don't feel safe doing. I promise you I won't be mad if you say no." I reached across the table and took her hand. "Up in a couple of towns that I work in there's a crazy high demand for prescription drugs, which got me thinkin' that that pharmacy where you work can be very lucrative for us."

"Believe it or not, bae, me and my coworker was just talking about this same thing the other day."

"Do you think she or he—yo' coworker—would be down for the cause?"

"If I do anything it's just going to be between me and you. I'ma think about it and have an answer for you before you leave in the morning," she said, makin' it clear to me that she wanted to wake up next to me. I did one better for her. I woke her up that next morning by slidin' balls deep in her from behind, then again while standing up in the shower.

Chapter 14

To lock everything in place with Georgia, I let her hold down the Camaro while I gave her Dodge Breeze the TLC that it was in very much need of. I really didn't care if her car fell apart, but I knew in her mind that she'd seen it as her man takin' care of her, which motivated her to try her damndest to do what's needed to take care of her man. Yeah, yeah, I know it seem like I was doin' what Georgia had said other guys had done to her in the past, but the difference with me is that she's gettin' something out of it. Man, if you think that you can survive in the cold-hearted streets without being a liar, manipulator, and—when push comes to shove—a merciless killer, then you're a damn fool. I can promise you that there's a nice cold body bag waiting on you and that life of a thug isn't for you. But shid, thug life isn't for anybody who thinks it's a game. Truth be told, none of us in the streets wanna live the way we do. We all crave that simple life—or our thug life.

With Georgia at work doing her homework on the best way to access the prescription pills gold mine without gettin' caught, and my uncle Curt hard at work giving her car the major tune-up and oil change it needed, I got out on my grind. My nigga—Shawn—called me, asking me did I have anything that I needed help doin' so he could earn him a few bucks. I knew he had just lost his job at Pizza Hut for hittin' his smart disrespectful mouth manager in the mouth. Because it happened off the clock, he was fired but because he didn't return to work after it happened, the spiteful manager put it down as he quit; so Shawn couldn't collect unemployment. Shawn was a good kid and I said that that way because he was only twenty and had no criminal record. I don't even remember how I met him in the first place. I think it was at the barber shop. All I know is that he's a good middleman. It was his side hustle when he wasn't makin' pizzas.

I didn't have anything for him to do for me at the time but I gave 'im $100 so that he'd have somethin' in his pocket. I let him ride with me; actually, I had him drive me around while I made my deliveries.

"AR, I got a guy who wants a couple of balls hard. I tax him two hundred dollars apiece for 'em. Do you think you can let me catch that?"

"Shawn, man, if you got money online always, go get that. I don't care what you tax a muthafucka, that's yo' thang. Just as long as I get the three hundred I need fo' 'em, I'm straight."

"Good lookin'," he said excitedly. Then headed to make the sale.

Man, the police pulled up on us as soon as Shawn went to make the sale in the West Allis apartment building. Nawl, it wasn't a setup or no snitch ass shit like that. The police just knew that a lot of dope fiends live in the building and took a chance on the two black guys in the fancy black Tahoe parked in an all-white neighborhood just might be a couple of dealers. So, full of suspicion, they parked and watched my truck. I saw 'em sitting back there and made sure I had everything put up just in case they decided to do more than just watch. What I couldn't prepare for was Shawn coming out of the building talking to his hype buddy. I don't know where the other squad car came from, but the two cars swooped in blocking the truck so I couldn't drive off if I wanted to, and jumped out, guns drawn at the three of us.

I kinda smirked and shook my head, knowing I was good and praying that Shawn wouldn't fold on me. The police did their searches. Myself and the truck were good; they searched Shawn and still found nothing. But they found the two balls of hard in the fiend's front pocket and his pipe in the back pocket of his dirty overalls. I wasn't worried about me because no matter what, the police knew I'd never gotten outta the truck and the fiend don't know me; the only person he knew is Shawn. Man, the police took two muthafuckas to jail that day and not who you'd expect. They took hype buddy for the drugs they found on him and me for a warrant that I didn't know I had. I was heated. After I'd done all of the bitchin' and moanin' about how they had it wrong, I reminded myself of the rules and instructed Shawn to hold down my whip, then I shut the hell up until I got to the jail where I could use the phone.

I called my BM because she was one of the main people who could explain to the police that I'd already been questioned and released for the incident at the club with me and my sister's crazy ex-boyfriend. When Rhonda answered, she told me that she was already on it because Shawn had answered my phone that I'd left in the truck and told Alexis what happened. Rhonda also told me that this time they had a $1,000 bail on me, but it couldn't be paid until they took me to Milwaukee County Jail where the warrant was issued. With that said, I knew there was nothin' else I could do but shut up and wait.

While I sat waiting to be transferred, Georgia had figured out just how to get large amounts of prescription drugs without bringing immediate heat onto herself. The coworker that she'd told me about was in charge of the pharmacy's inventory. Over lunch, the coworker had confessed to her that she'd been half assing her duties by just recopying the same inventory sheet. She said she did it because it rarely changed, and when it does change it stays that way for months. Georgia knew by her coworker doing things that way, that the pharmacy's inventory records were already fucked up. After their lunch break, Georgia made her way to a computer and placed a triple order for delivery. After she'd finished manipulating the order, she went about her work with a smile thinking about how pleased I'd be with her and how she would spend the extra money that I'd promised her.

From everything that I'd shown her about my character, there wasn't a bit of doubt that I wouldn't do what I said. By the end of her work day, Georgia had decided that she would spend whatever I paid her on new clothes and shoes since she now had a reason to dress up.

Chapter 15

This tall, skinny, young white guy that was in the cramped holding cell with me was mumbling and laughin' as he paced back a forth. He didn't look like he was crazy, even though the nut-case was dressed in a green Army jacket, a T-shirt with a big yellow smiley printed on the front of it, some rumpled dark blue jeans and a new lookin' pair of brown and blue hiking boots. I asked him was he alright.

"Oh, yeah, man. I'm just going over something for my show later. I do standup comedy. I'm sure you haven't heard of me, but in case you have, my name is Buddy Pal."

"Well, I don't have nothin' else to do but sit and wait. I like to laugh and with this bullshit I'm going through right now I can use something to take my mind off of it. So, hell, let me hear some of what you got."

"Man, just so you understand, I don't really tell jokes. I tell stories and most people laugh at me, some people beat me up, but most of the time they laugh. You're a pretty nice size guy and you're black, so that tells me that you're no stranger to doing time. So if at any point during me telling my story you get the urge to punch out a goofy looking white boy, wait until the guard comes by with the keys so we can bust up outta here." He chuckled, going right into his act.

The Machine Gun Kelly lookin' comic had me laughing my ass off especially with the story he finished with.

"I love black women. I like all of the colors of the rainbow but black women just make me feel like a man's man. I love me a hood chick. I'm married to one right now with one of them big earthquake booties. I can see you know what I'm talking about. Well, Latisha and I aren't really married but we've been together for years, you know how that goes. We gotta pretty happy life when we're together. We have five and a half children. Why you laughing, I'm serious. One of my daughters was born without legs. My wife named her Halfa Pal. Halfa is a real sweet girl, she's smart and tough, and she don't mind getting her hands dirty. . .

Latisha and I have a very strange relationship. Strange like our instant family. I've been trying to figure out for years now, how do I got five and a half babies with her. Honestly, I'd never had full sex with her until after the last kid was born. By that time, I believe Latisha felt obligated to give me some pussy. Why not? I do my part as a man. I make sure there's food, that her hair and nails are done, that all the bills are paid and I'm current on my child support . . .

Child support—that's another thing that puzzles me about our relationship. Why am I still paying child support when all of our kids are grown, most with kids of their own. Well, everybody except the last one, Halfa. She's nineteen but has a little more maturing to do before I'm comfortable letting her go out and finding her better half . . .

I'm not much of a drinker, but my wife is. Man, she loves herself some wine. I'm telling she loves it so much, that our little house in the heart of the ghetto has a vineyard growing in the backyard. Pretty much on any given Sunday you can find Latisha in the backyard blasting the song, *Walk It Out* and dancing barefoot in a tub of grapes . . .

You know, I never used to question our family ties until one Sunday when we were keeping all of our ugly ass grandkids. I know, I know that's not nice, but I'm just being honest. My children are beautiful, but their offspring. Those little mutherfuckers are *Walking Dead* zombie ugly . . ."

Dawg, man, I was laughing so hard that I was low-key mad when the officer came and told me that my warrant had been dropped and I was free to go. I got Bobby's information and told him that I would come see his show later that night. The police allowed me to make a free call. I remembered Rhonda tellin' me that Shawn had answered my phone when she called, so I tried my luck and got lucky. He answered the phone for me. I told him that I was released and for him to come scoop me from the Taco Bell across the street from the police station. Before I left, I found out that Bobby Pal's bail was only $150; I paid the bone for him.

"Aye, Bobby? When I get to the club my first bottle's on you, right?"

"Yeah, sure. Better yet the whole show's on me. I'll leave your name at the door!" he said, still locked in the holding cell, waiting for the bond to be processed. "Man, you didn't have to do that. Latisha is on her way. She should be walking through the door any second now."

"That's a real person?" I asked in surprise. And just as I was walkin' out, a fine full-figured black woman was walkin' in. I started to ask her was her name Latisha but with all that ass that she was swinging behind her, I knew it was. As soon as I dropped in the passenger seat of my truck, Shawn told me that RG had seen my truck and pulled up on him askin' for me. He told him that I was locked up on some bullshit and that I'd be out as soon as I got to the Milwaukee County jail. Shawn went on to say that RG had paid 'im to take him over by Bo's spot to cop some work. I wasn't trippin' on that because both Big Bo and RG are my guys. I was geek to hear that Bo had some wurk than anything because I was almost out, and like I said, the streets were drying up after that big Fed bust.

The reason I was so geek that Bo had it was because I knew he wouldn't tax me all that much and because Bo really only pushed heroin through, every now and then he'd move a few dozen kilos of coke for the hell of it. Bo really didn't have to hustle anymore. He had more than enough money and good businesses for him to chill, but he was like most big ballin' ass niggas that's still in the game. He was in love with the power of it all. More like addicted to it.

I made a mental note to ride down on Bo the next day to check out what he had. While we were heading back on our side of the city, I got a call from Georgia on her way home from work. She told me that she had some good news and some great news for me. From the excitement in her voice I had a good guess what it was about. I told her I'll meet her at her crib and she can tell me then because it wasn't a conversation for the phone.

I'd overheard Shawn on the phone with his girl and knew that he wanted to go spend some of that money that he made on her. So I decided to let 'im hold down the Tahoe. I was a young niggah once. I know how it is, so why not let him go kick it with his chick in style!

"Lil' bro, take me over by the garage so I can pick this girl car up from Uncle Curt and take it back to her so she can come up off my Camaro. I don't want her ass to get to comfortable with it an' shit. Yo' ass don't get too comfortable with this here either. I'ma let you hold my baby down but I'ma be callin' yo' ass early in the morning for my bitch back and I don't want a tiny blemish on her or that's yo' ass, Mr. Postman!" I made a joke but Shawn knew the threat was real and promised that he would take care of it, then dropped me off.

Calls started flooding in, so I made a few deliveries on my way to Georgia's. Uncle Curt had her car running like it was brand new. I knew she would be happy with it the next time she got behind the wheel. When I pulled onto her parking lot, I called her down to the car because I knew she had plans for me to stay with her, and that wasn't gonna happen because I still had paper to chase. Besides that, I'd made plans to talk my BM to see my man's—Bobby Pal's—comedy show later.

After Georgia told me her genius plan to get the drugs I wanted in the large amounts, she knew I needed to make it all worth it. I explained to her what happened to me earlier that day and for it I really had to put in some extra work to make up for the lost time. She tried to convince me that she didn't mind if I came over late. I told her that I didn't want her waiting up and being all tired at work when I know I'm not going to come back. Hell, she knew that she wasn't my only one, just like she knew that she ain't my number one. But I wasn't gonna be a fool and tell her that I wanted to spend time with Rhonda. I don't care what type of understandin' you've got with a female, tellin' her that you're not going to come lay up with her so you can lay up with someone else would make a broad go crazy on you. But if you think you got pimp in you, do it and let me know how it worked out for you.

 Before I was all the way out of the parking lot after gettin' my whip back from Georgia, I was on the phone with Rhonda telling her to get sexy for me so I can take her out. She surprised me when she suggested that we take my sister out with us. I was surprised because she don't usually like to share the time that she gets with me. I agreed, and that was the end of the conversation. Rhonda promptly told me to get off the phone so she can start gettin' ready. Like two minutes later, Alexis texted me asking what time was I coming to pick her up. I remembered Bobby tellin' me that he was the closing act so I told her about 8:30, to be on the safe side.

Chapter 16

While my sister was enjoyin' life, that head-case King Tivon was still going through it. After spending a few days stacking Alexis's temporarily abandoned social media pages, something finally popped up that caught his attention. Tyneil was about to be doing a photoshoot down in Chicago. The reason the news of the porn actress had caught his attention is because he knew that she's sis cousin and knew that Tyneil would know where she is if she wasn't hiding out at Tyneil's place in Milwaukee. KT hurried up and booked the soonest flight that he could get to Chicago, then headed to the airport. Before boarding the plane, he stopped in the airport's gift shop and bought cheap toyish binoculars.

A few hours later, he was driving a big black tinted out SUV through the streets of downtown Chicago, heading toward Tyneil's lakefront photoshoot. He wasn't worried 'bout being seen at the photoshoot because it was being done outdoors in a public place and he knows it would be a nice sized crowd 'cause people love watchin' things like that. But since he wasn't just some any ol' body, KT still had to dress down. He dressed in plain dark denim jeans, a dark colorful Polo shirt and a pair of Air Jordan's. Just befo' he got out of the truck, he added dark Prada shades and a Chicago baseball cap that he pulled down low and slightly to the right on his head, helping him hide his face without lookin' suspect.

The punk got lucky and caught Tyneil's shoot right away. While he stood in the crowd waiting for her to finish, he used the binoculars to scan the faces of the crowd, looking for Lexi. When he didn't find her out there nowhere, he decided instead of givin' up the element of surprise that he had by questioning Tyneil, he would just follow her for a while in hopes that she lead him to his obsession. With that decided, KT smiled.

Just befo' it got dark outside, King Tivon was five cars behind Tyneil's lil' powder blue Mercedes heading up I-94 back to Milwaukee. Once there, he followed her across the city into Brown Deer where she turned inside the gated parking lot to her condominium. He slowed up and watched her taillights until they were out of sight, then he parked and jogged back to the building where he climbed the gate and briskly walked to the rear of the parking lot. There he found Tyneil's car parked in its assigned spot.

Crouching so that he wouldn't be seen, he used the binoculars to scan the windows of the condominium. He caught sight of Tyneil on the upper floor standin' by what he assumed was her bedroom window. After a moment, she pulled the blinds closed, leavin' him looking at her sexy silhouette as she undressed. A little while later, Tyneil came back out of the building dressed in a different outfit. She got in her car and headed off. KT had to wait in the shadows 'til she was off the parking lot to move or risk her seeing him. As soon as she was gone, he ran through the gate befo' it closed and made him have to climb back over it. By the time he'd made it back to his ride, she was gone. Had he been just a lil' faster, Tyneil would've led him right to Lexi, who had invited her to come out with us.

Chapter 17

After finishing up my rounds, I bought an outfit for the night and headed straight to Rhonda's to get dressed. I made my way into the bedroom where she was puttin' on eyeshadow. Rhonda has a shapely full figure and a creamy brown skin that I can't keep my hands off. As I stood there watching my sexy queen standing with her back to me, her juicy booty covered in the thin lacy fabric panties, her bare thick legs and little barefoot kicked up a strong desire in me to cum inside her. We still had an hour before we had to pick up my sister and get to the club, so I moved in for a quickie.

She must've sensed my presence behind her, she looked up and met my eyes in the mirror. Her curious smile quickly turned to a knowin' grin as the tip of my hardness slid inside her panties and between her firm her ass cheeks. The friction created by me slowly pushing my length across her skin sent tingles through my body. Rhonda gasped, as I reached down and stroked the Ms. Kitty tattoo on her thigh with my fingertips. Her head rolled back, resting on my chest, and she closed her eyes as I dragged my hand slowly up her leg on my way to my targeted destination. Rhonda parted her legs a little wider, and she arched her back, poking her ass out as my touch reached the top of her inner thigh. Lookin' in her face through the mirror with her sweet lips slightly open, my hand stroked the hairless flesh of her warm mound.

I parted her lower lips, and her wetness dripped, coating my fingers as I ran my finger over the top of her clit, then down through her silky folds. I loved the sound of her panting and the way she pushed her mound harder onto my hand, encouraging me to go deeper. I pushed two of my fat fingers in her warm hole, and she went into a hot frenzy. She reached with one hand and took hold of my length, stroking it fast. Rhonda's stroking sent waves of pleasure through my body. I moved my free hand up her body and cupped her breasts one by one and lightly pinched her swollen nipples, heightening her arousal.

Bending over, she released my hardness and braced herself with her hands on the vanity. Lockin' eyes with her through the mirror, I kicked her legs wider apart, giving myself unrestricted access, then I pushed all the way in her warmth. She moaned as she reached up and cupped the back of my head, and I feverishly went to pounding her from behind until we both climaxed. An hour or so later, we were seated at the comedy club with my sister, and Tyneil my stalker.

Bobby Pal had us all laughin' our asses off. I'm laughing even harder because I know the woman who he's talkin' about is sittin' two tables over from us. When he came to the part of the story where we left off at when I got released, he stopped and pointed me out. I don't know if you've ever been to a live comedy show or not, but it's never a good thing when the comic points you out.

"Now, now ladies and guys. I need to pause right there and tell you how I met that guy right there." He pointed and they put the spotlight on our table for a moment. "So a few hours before the show I was locked in a cage with that big angry black guy right there. Sure he looks nice and calm now that he's at the table with not one but three hot chicks. But he wasn't all smiley faced when he was thrown— No, *I* was thrown in the cell the cops escorted him in. I'd seen a few rose petals dropped at his feet. I'm serious. He looked so scary the damn guards didn't even want to ask him his name

. . .

As you see, I'm a tall guy, 6'4" but I don't have any weight on me. Now look at him." They put the spotlight on me again. "He's built like a King Silverback in human clothes. I got as far as I could away from him in the tiny cell and started praying that wife made it there with the bail money before he notices me in the room. When suddenly that man turns to me and says, *Aye, white boy, you al'ight*? I damn near piss my pants. I was so scared but I remembered my wife telling me that if I don't show fear they won't attack. At the time she was talking about our grandkids, but I figured it might work for him as well. I didn't know how to respond to him so I introduced myself, *Hi, my name is Bobby Pal and I do standup comedy*. He says, *Yeah, I like comedy. You make me laugh now*! I couldn't think straight. My mind was all over the place. Suddenly, I was an awkward kid again being shoved inside a locker in gym class. My mind stopped on the basics and I blurted out, Knock knock."

I jumped up outta my seat and said, "Really! You gon' stand there and do me like that?" Once again the spotlight was put on me. I couldn't do nothin' but drop and shake my head, laughing at myself because I knew he had got me. "That's not what happened," I said, then dropped back in my seat laughing along with him and everyone else. Bobby Pal went on and truthfully explained how things really went, then moved back into tellin' the story about his grandkids. Now you have to understand that Bobby Pal couldn't have been no more than thirty years old, so he was way too young to have grandkids, which made everything even funnier.

"Now back to my little evil foul mouth grandkids. I got three of them. There's three of them lil' sonuvbitches by the way. A girl that's ten and two boys ages seven and four. So the Sunday afternoon that made me question everything, it had to have been close to a million degrees outside. It was so damn hot, I went on the porch for like thirty seconds and my shadow started sweating . . .

I took a look out behind the house and as always the wife was in the yard, drunk as the Milwaukee river walking it out in her bucket of hooch . . .

Cici, my helpful granddaughter, took it upon herself to go in the refrigerator and pour herself and her little cousins some nice tall glasses of grandma's grape juice. I would like to believe that she did not know what she was doing . . . but she added crushed ice to it, and sat out salted peanuts . . .

I didn't see any of this because I sitting in my bedroom smoking and tryna alphabetize my blunt wraps. 'Cause you know, not every wrap goes good with every type of weed. Now in the midst of doing that, I started to wonder who was the genius that alphabetized the alphabet. When suddenly my granddaughter burst staggering into the room, mad as hell and says, '*Papa, you need to go in there and get Halfa 'cause the bitch in there running around talking to me like I'm her child. I told the bitch that my Mama at Jim's working the North track. Papa, you better get her before I smack her ass!*'

I almost died laughing. I couldn't believe what I was hearing. I pulled myself together and said, '*Little girl watch your mouth. Young ladies don't talk like that.*' Before I could go on, she sharply replied, '*Young ladies don't but I'ma bad bitch like my Mama and my Granny.*' She corrected me complete with a head roll and a finger snap.

I had no response for that. I choked back my laughter and explained to the little monster, that it was mother who asked her auntie to look after her until she returned from the gym, working out on the treadmill and that she shouldn't lie on her aunt because I know that Halfa isn't in there running around anywhere . . .

Just like that, the little witch growled and snapped on me. '*Gurrrrrh! You always standing up with her when you need to make her stand up for herself like my Mama do me. I'ma go tell my Granny, she'll make Halfa stand toe to toe with me since you're good for nothin'!*' She stormed back out of the room. I yelled *good luck with that* behind her and went back to smoking. A few minutes later, I hear the boys running through the house banging things around and making a ruckus. I yelled, *Hey, you two bad asses, stop running in this house. Go outside with that*! The next thing I know, my grandsons come in just stumbling and staggering into the bedroom. Please keep in mind that I'm at least an ounce of weed in by my lonesome. I'm high as the clouds in a clear blue sky. So when I looked at them I noticed that they're both fucked up. I mean their clothes were ripped and dirty, the seven-year-old has a nice golf ball size knot on his forehead and a busted lip. The four-year-old has a black eye that's damn near closed. Seeing them like that, my high was damn near blown. I'm, like, *Good God, what happened to you two*? The seven-year-old nonchalantly wipes the blood away with the back of his hand that's leaking from his busted lip and says, '*Papa, we—we had to come to an understanding with tee-tee Halfa's fast ass about comin' at us sideways. But, Papa, don't worry 'bout that. Me, you and us,*' he said, pointing back over his shoulder at the four-year-old, who I at that time noticed was holding a fully loaded water gun in one hand and a little hard plastic baseball bat in the other. The seven-year-old went on, '*—need to have a heart to man talk 'cause the block is too hot to be outside right now.*' Again I almost piss myself laughing so hard. I said, *Junior, I think you mean, we need to have a heart to heart or a man to man talk. I don't know how to have a heart to man talk.*

I shouldn't have corrected him because the four-year-old quickly stepped up, rapidly squeezing his trigger, shooting me repeatedly in the leg and said, '*You not talkin' when he talkin'. Talk again and it's face shots, Papa!*' I immediately shut the fuck up and threw my hands up in surrender. Not a mock surrender either; I was serious. The lil' goon had filled his gun up in the mop bucket or something because I could smell bleach and my jeans were fading where I'd been shot in the leg. So you're damn right I shut up and listen, I don't want to get bleach in my eyes.

'*Papa, Papa, put your hands down, white boy, it's all love here,*' the seven-year-old said and that's when I questioned everything about my life with Latish. Sitting on the bed staring at the spout of my four-year-old grandson's gun, I knew the only way for me to make it out unharmed was to do as my wife taught me to do when dealing with my grandkids alone. I swallowed my fear and said, *Boys, how about we all take a breather, let's go in the kitchen, have a eat at the bar, drink some milk and sip on some cookies . . .*

Hey, sometimes you have to speak in a language that they understand. Thank you! That's my time."

Chapter 18

Letting Shawn hold down my truck is where I kinda fucked up with him. Like I said, I did it so my lil' guy could impress and kick it with his girl; that's it, that's all. What I'd unknowingly done was fuel his lust to be one of the big boys. Remember, Shawn's not a thug or a hardcore hustler. He's a good goal-minded dude that has a typa swagger about him that makes it easy for him to mingle with niggahs on the level so that he could middleman the connection needed to move whatever lands in his lap. But after spending the whole day whipping around in my fully custom Tahoe, he'd made his mind up that he wanted to get fully in the game.

While I was at the comedy club laughing my ass off, Shawn was out cruising the city with his girlfriend's older rogue ass brother, Tone. Shawn always found himself tryna impress Tone so he could stop lookin' down on him. Yeah, at the time Shawn was in between job, but when he's working and doing his lil' side-hustle he was always doing better than Tone and just couldn't see it. Tone was anything special. He was a thief that hit a bunch of small licks that kept a few bucks in his pocket and fresh kicks on his feet, but he wasn't a stacker like Shawn. Tone always went for instant gratification instead. On the low, he envied my lil' niggah because Tone knew that nobody who knew him in their right mind would ever trust him the way I trust Shawn.

As Shawn whipped through the streets lookin' for somethin' to get into or in between, Tone sparked up a blunt and muted the radio so they could talk.

"Man, I was just sittin' over here thinking 'bout what you told me that went down with you and bro today."

"Yeah, that was fucked up," Shawn replied reachin' for the blunt. "But what about it though?"

"The way we're livin' out here right now ain't it. It ain't nothin' but a matter of time befo' we get knocked and be sittin' in a cell broke as a bitch, with nothin' to show for it. When we can easily be whippin' big boy trucks like this that's ours if we get on our hustle fo'real fo'real."

"All that sounds sweet as a bitch. I feel like a boss drivin' this pretty muthfucka," Shawn replied as he found a place to park so they could go check out what's shaking in this lil' hole-in-the-wall strip club over on the South side. "If we had the cash, I know where we can get some good wurk from. But the niggah Bo don't do nothin' smaller than a ounce."

"Bro, I ain't talking 'bout copin' a funky ass ounce. I'm tryna cop somethin' that would have us ridin' in something phat like this here with the first couple of flips. Shawn, man, if you think about it, that's all AR be doing. He buy a car in one flip and put it together with the next one or two—"

"See, Tone, that's where you're wrong. Big bro bag so fat because of his ability to never run out of wurk. As long as he got wurk, he can do what he wanna do. I've seen him buy a car and have it all done up and he didn't do it on no payment plan shit like you think he does. I know him. AR do what he wants the way he wants. When he bought his van, he slapped it in the shop to have it done the way he wanted it before he took it home. Don't be fooled, bro got that paper fo'real."

"Well, fuck all that! I know a lick that can get us the bread we need to put us in the game. I've been kinda peepin' it out fo' a few weeks. I ain't hit it yet because it's at least a two-man job and I need something big to move the merch in."

"Somethin' big like that U-Haul over there?" Shawn pointed to the medium size box-truck parked on the street across from where they were sitting.

"Exactly like that," Tone said, tryna keep the excitement out of his voice. Tone knew that he'd pretty much hooked Shawn; now he had to reel 'im on in. "Niggah, if you got heart to bust this move with me, I'll go steal that muthafucka and we can go get this poppin' right now?"

"I'm down fo' whudeva. Go do yo' thang. I'm tired of livin' on the edge of being broke. Shit, only two things can happen when we do this. We end up in jail or we be put in the game."

"Say nomo!" Tone said, then slipped outta the truck and vanished into the shadows of the night.

Like five minutes later, Shawn all of a sudden saw the U-Haul truck recklessly take off down the street. He quickly spun my truck around and followed it, knowin' that it was Tone behind the wheel just from the way it was being driven. In Shawn's mind he had reached the point of either going big or going home. There was no middle ground for him. Talkin' on the phone, Tone told him that it would be best if he followed him down to the spot in Racine just in case they had to ditch the U-Haul and run.

Shawn agreed and followed him to the location. After riding by it and circling the block, he found a place to park that was a safe distance away so that my truck wouldn't get mixed up in anything. Then he climbed in the U-Haul with Tone so they could get it done and over with before he allowed his second thoughts get the best of him.

"Man, listen, I know you over there shaking in yo boots," Tone said, breaking the silence as he drove slowly through the neighborhood of the location that he had planned for them to hit. "But shake that shit off. I'm tellin' you this easy money. The key to it is doing it fast. I know you ain't tryna get caught like I ain't, brotha-in-law." He laid it on thick, makin' Shawn feel accepted by him while tryna think of a way get over on him.

"I'm good, I'm ready," Shawn said as they turned onto the poorly lit, deserted lot.

"When I crash this muthafucka through the garage door, man, just start grabbing stuff and throwing it in back of the U-Haul. If you can, don't grab nothin' cheap and slang that shit in the truck. Niggahs don't care 'bout the condition of the boxes, just the condition of what's inside 'em."

"Man, man, man, we both here fo' the same thang, so shut up and let's get to it!" Shawn exclaimed in a hoarse nervous voice.

On that note, Tone turned the truck in the opposite direction of the small car audio and rim shop's garage door, then promptly stomped the gas pedal to the floor. The U-Haul shot backwards, ramming straight through the door. Both of them were movin' so fast that they were out of the truck and inside the building before the sound of the loud crash had diminished. They quickly started grabbin' boxes of rims, both knowing the bigger the rim the better, and tossing them into the back of the truck. Shawn rushed over and started grabbing boxes of radios, amps, TVs and whuteva, knowin' he could sell those items real fast. While he was behind the counter, he came across a little black money pouch with a padlock on it. As he stuffed it in his waist, he felt the thickness of the pouch and knew it was filled with cash.

"Man, we gotta enough! Let's go! Let's go!" Tone yelled after tossin' what he had in his arms in the back of the truck and slamming its door closed, making sure to latch it so it wouldn't come open on 'em as they drove, then he got in the driver's seat and started pulling away.

Shawn took off running to catch him, thinking that he was tryna leave him there. But Tone was moving slow enough that Shawn was able to get in the passenger seat still. As Tone sped away from the store, Shawn decided then and there that he would keep the money pouch to himself. His idea was to spilt whatever amount inside of it up with me for some dope when he hooked up with me later that morning and use the rest to buy a car.

They both were laughing excitedly as they raced away. Tone let Shawn out by my truck and Shawn got in and followed him onto the highway and back to the Mil. They got off the highway on the North side a few miles from where they live and pulled over so they could come up with someplace to stash the stuff and get rid of the stolen U-Haul. That's when I received a text from Shawn asking me for my uncle Doc's number. I knew as soon as I'd seen the message that Shawn had somethin' up.

My uncle, Doc, may he rest in peace, was one of the truest hardcore hustlers I've ever known. And that says a lot, seeing that I come from a whole entire family of hustlers, whores, pimps, and drug dealers. I gave the lil' nigga the number and told him to be at my crib to pick me up about 10 or 10:30 later that morning because it was almost 1 o'clock in the morning. Rhonda saw me tapping away on my phone and caught a lil' attitude, thinkin' I was about to try to leave her and snapped on me.

"Niggah, I hope you don't think you're leaving this house tonight! No, sir, babe. This is my time with you, so you can tell that crackhead or chickenhead bitch that you ain't coming and turn that damn phone off!"

"Whoa, Luv, I ain't goin' nowhere. That was Shawn. I let him drive my truck and he was just checkin' in with me. So stop tryna beat me up." I explained with a smile.

"I'm finna go take a shower. I expect you to be ready to beat this pussy up when I get out." She knows her jazziness turns me on. So I got up and joined her in the shower.

Chapter 19

Shawn paid Doc a hundred bucks to park the U-Haul in his enclosed driveway so it wouldn't be easily found. Besides, everyone in his hood knows that there're cameras on his house so nobody even thought 'bout fuckin' with his spot. To be safer still, my uncle put a padlock on the truck and gave a key to Shawn, because as I said, nobody in their right mind would trust Tone. The niggah just had shiesty written all over his face; it was unc's first time meeting the niggah and he didn't trust him in the slightest. He made sure that Tone had seen that he kept a heat on him always.

Shawn dropped Tone off at the crib that he stay in with his sister, who—if you recall me sayin'—is Shawn's girlfriend. So when he didn't get out, Tone questioned why wasn't he stayin' over. Shawn told him that he had to get up early to scoop me up and give me my truck back. He promised to be there to pick him up around noon so they can go get started on movin' their merch.

"My OG will let me use his car so we'll have a way to move around. Everything straight. Doc good people. He ain't gonna fuck with nothin'."

"Al'ight then," Tone said, feelin' a bit reluctant as he went in the house.

When Shawn made it home, he immediately cut the bottom of the money pouch open and counted out the cash that was in it. The cash totaled approximately $8,700 in mostly small bills. Smiling like a kid in a toy store, Shawn plotted out his plan for the money. He put away $1,200 fo' a rainy day, put $500 in his pocket to fuck off with, and set the remaining 7 geez aside for me, hoping that I'd take it for the Cadillac that I had for sale. I know it sound like my lil' guy was on some instant gratification shit himself, by the way he'd planned spending the money out, but he wasn't. I already had a nice sound system in the Cadillac, so he really didn't have to do anything to it, but if he did want to add to it or change it up, he had a whole U-Haul full of brand new car audio stuff and rims to choose from. He did plan on upgrading the 20s I had put on it to some 24s or maybe 26s out of the merch that they had. Then once they sold enough of the merch, he would do as planned and invest that cash in some wurk and be on from there.

His ass was so geeked up he couldn't sleep. When I pulled up to my crib at about 9:45 a.m., my truck was parked out there freshly washed and waxed with his ass knocked the fuck out in the driver's seat.

"Wake yo' scary ass up!" I yelled while knockin' on the window, startling him awake.

"Damn, man, I ain't even know I was asleep," he said, getting out of the truck.

"Lil' bro, if I didn't trust you I wouldn't have gave you my whip. You didn't have to sleep in it outside of my house. You could've taken it home." I teased him while lookin' my truck over to make sure it wasn't damaged.

"Man, fuck you. I just got here like ten minutes ago!" he retorted, then went right into explaining what he'd done with Tone and in the same breath askin' me how much would I let him get the Cadillac for.

"Let's go scoop the niggah Tone up right quick 'cause I know his ass over there going crazy waitin' on you to come get 'im so y'all can divide up the merch. When I see what all y'all got, we can probably make a trade for the car."

"Bet!"

We got the truck parked and got in my van, then zoomed over to Tone's, got him and Lala, who's Shawn's girlfriend, then went to Doc's crib. Unc ass was in the backyard firing up the grill with his kids and three of his hoes when we pulled up. He also had the back of the U-Haul open with his hoes emptying it out and stackin' everything in neat piles on the ground. He explained to Shawn and Tone that he wants the stolen truck away from his spot as soon as possible and assured them that everything that was in it was all stack right there where they could see it. But both Doc and I knew that wasn't the truth. There was no way my good hustlin' ass uncle was gonna only accept $100 when he had a truck full of thousands of dollars' worth of stolen merchandise. Merchandise that he could tell from the way it had been thrown in the back of the truck that neither Shawn nor Tone knew how much they actually had. I also knew that him havin' his girls unload the truck was a distraction to help his lie. But I wasn't sayin' shit about it to 'im. It wasn't my stuff.

Later, after everything was all done with and it was just me and him, Unc told me that he'd taken two sets of rims, some TVs, amps and subwoofers for his troubles. Anyways, my cousin—Blacc—gave Shawn and Tone their first sale of the day. Tone, being thirsty fo' some cash, allowed Cuzo to give him $2,500 and 3 pounds of loud for a set of 28-inch rims, a subwoofer box with three 15" inch Kicker L7 subs in it, and a 7" inch screen in-dash radio. After overhearing the deal that I made with Shawn for the two sets of rims, one a set of 24s and the other a set of 26s, a couple of in-dash screen radios long with amps and speakers, for the Cadillac, Doc tossed a similar proposition Tone's way.

"Say, Tone, I know you tryna be out here ridin' somethin' big?"

"An' you know it!" Tone excitedly agreed.

"See that 96 Impala over there." Doc pointed toward the car. "That's mine but it can be yours for say two thousand bucks and a pound of that kush you just got?" Seeing the look that he was hoping for in Tone's eyes, unc went on, "Just look at it. I got it lifted already and everything. I know 24s will go right on it, maybe 26s. I know you got rims for it already but if you want I'll throw in the ones I got for it. I just gotta go get 'em from over at my other spot. I just had the car painted and just ain't had the time to put the rims on it yet. I was puttin' it together to sell and since my hoes love to smoke I thought we could make a deal?"

"Hell yeah, we can! How do that bitch run though?" Tone said, following unc over to the Impala.

"Oh she snot. I just put on a new rear end so it's got positive traction and a full tune-up," Uncle Doc said, pressing the remote start button and making the car growl to life. That's all Tone needed to hear for the deal to be made.

When it was all over and done with, Shawn and Tone both ended up with nice whips, 9 ounces of dope each, 2 pounds of kush that Shawn still split evenly with Tone after Tone had given the third pound away for the car. Shawn knew he couldn't trip about it because he had kept all of the money from the cash pouch. So the way he saw it was that they were even. They both had over 10 geez in their pockets as well, so everyone was happy. Even Lala because her man bought a 2003 Dodge Neon from me for her, and her brother put a set of white and chrome 18" inch rims on it to set the little white car off. So, like I said, everyone was happy.

Chapter 20

So, after Shawn and nem were gone to get started on their climbs to the next levels in the game, I was selling Tyneil a set of 22s for her car. I had her come over to Uncle Doc's crib since the rims that I'd sold her was a set outta the ones that he'd taken from the boys and he offered to put 'em on for her, which meant that I wouldn't have to get my hands dirty. Win-win fo' me. What I didn't know was that Tyneil was being followed.

King Tivon had come back to Tyneil's place at around seven that morning and staked it out until she left to do what she had to do. He followed her to the post office, then to Walmart. When Tyneil went inside the store, he pulled into the parking space behind her car and waited for her to come out almost an hour or so later. Tyneil not once paid the truck parked behind her any mind as she put her bags in the back seat of her car.

When she took the shopping cart back over to the rack, she ran into Lala who's one of her aunt's personal caregivers at the senior living home that she's in. That's how Tyneil learned that I had rims for sale and all I'd done was have Doc put 'em on the car that I'd sold Shawn. Anyway, if it wasn't for that conversation with Lala, Tyneil would've led KT to Lexi after leavin' Walmart, but since I told her that I didn't have all day to be waitin' on her, she quickly dropped her grocery bags off at home and came straight to where I was to get the rims for her car. Even if it wasn't for the rims,

Tyneil would've still ditched going to the gun range with my sister and Rhonda to come hang out with me. The gun range was my BM's idea. She felt that both of the girls needed to get used to the feel of shooting a gun so the next time a situation came up where they would have to handle one, they wouldn't be afraid to use it.

Needless to say, when KT pulled over to keep his eye on Tyneil, he spotted me. You know the punk instantly got heated. But from our first encounter, the nigga knew I stayed with a heat on me. An' since it never crossed his deranged mind that he would need one, he failed to pick one up from one of his guys in Chicago or to get one from one of his rogue family members in Milwaukee. So all he could do was sit fuming and stare me down from a safe distance.

But while doing that, he'd peeped me palming the voluptuous ass of this bad lil' Latina named Fetty, when I came and got my uncle's three-year-old daughter from her. Fetty fine ass was one of Doc's hoes, more or less. She was a young runaway from New York somewhere I think. I don't know how she ended in the Mil, but I know she was seventeen when she was introduced to Unc two years and some befo' I met her. I would never fuck with her because she was one of my uncle's girls but that didn't stop me from playfully flirting and coping a feel every now and then.

Nawl, my Doc didn't give a fuck. He knew it was harmless horseplay between me and his girls. Plus, like I said, he was a true player, pimp, and hustler. If you go look any one of those words up in the Real Niggah Dictionary, Doc's picture would be right there beside them.

Now no longer focused on Tyneil, but me instead, King Tivon came up with a scheme to hurt me by hurting my girl whom he assumed Fetty was. Knowing that he could catch up with Tyneil whenever, since he knows where she lives and what kinda car she drives, he abandoned his stakeout and followed Fetty to the corner store a few blocks away on 35th Street. Like I said, she was a hoe so she liked to walk so she could catch a trick or a dope boy that she could suck and fuck a few bills out of to bring home to daddy. When KT saw Fetty sauntering out of the store, he hurried up and rode down on her befo' she got too far.

"Damn, you sexy. What's your name, beautiful?" he asked from the window of his truck. When Fetty didn't break her stride or even glance his way, he popped at her again. "Come on, don't do me like that, can you slow up so I can park and get out to talk to you for a minute? I'm not from your city, I'm out here on business and I'm just tryna make a friend." That made her stop and look at him. So he turned on his flasher, doubled parked the ruck and got out. "Can I get your name now, beautiful?" he asked, seductively lickin' his lips.

Fetty took a moment to look him over. Though he was wearing his cap low and sunglasses, he looked familiar to her.

"It's Fetty," she told him her name, giving him a meekish smile.

"Fatty, I can see why they call you that with all that you got behind you."

"Not *Fatty*. Fetty, F-E-T-T-Y," she spelled it out for him, then giggled and explained to him that Fetty was short for Fetalia, as she texted Unc and told him that she caught her one and won't be coming right back to the house right away.

"My bad Fetty. I'm King—"

"Tivon," she finished for him. "Oooh my God! I can't believe it. When you got out of your truck I thought you looked familiar. You're King Tivon, I can't fuckin' believe I'm standing here talk to you right now!" she said excitedly.

Seein' her excitement, he offered her a hug; when she accepted it, he pulled her close and grabbed her ass. When she didn't complain, he tested her integrity a bit further.

"Ma, since you know who I am you know I can't just be standin' out here like this, so let's get in the truck and take a ride?"

"Yeah, I know who you are but you need to know that I'm not some silly bubble head fan who's going to just go with you and let you bust me down. If I get in that truck you need to understand that my time is money. Now, if that's not somethin' that you can get with, thank you for lettin' me meet you and I hope you enjoyed the hug."

KT wasn't expecting her to say anything close to what she had. But staying focused on gettin' his revenge, he reached in his pocket and pulled out a nice size knot of cash and counted out a gee for her.

"I hear you, ma, here's a stack, I hope it's enough for you to be my tour guide and to get your head where I would like it to be?" he said, holding the money out to her.

"I can work my magic with that," Fetty agreed, plucking the money outta his hand and stuffing it in the pocket of her tight jeans before climbin' in the passenger seat of his truck.

When KT got in and pulled out into traffic, Fetty immediately unzipped his pants and stuck her warm hand inside his boxers. Then she went to rubbing his length until it began hardening. What she didn't know was King Tivon's arousal wasn't from her touch but from his deranged thoughts of gettin' back at me. A moment later, when he was nice and firm, she freed his hardness and immediately went to sucking him. Befo' he could bust, Fetty suddenly stopped and peeled off her jeans. Now she was sitting in the passenger seat with nothing on from the waist down and her legs spread wide, with one foot up on the dash, playing with herself for his viewing pleasure. Wanting to know how wet she was, he slipped two of his fingers inside her pouty opening. Fetty moaned and he finger-fucked her faster. She put on her best show fo' him, moaning louder as she came all over his hand. When the nut-case finally pulled the truck over, he took her in the backseat where his real fun began.

Chapter 21

Man, I miss my vans! I had two at the same time, one Chevy and one Ford, both of 'em full-sized. I loved my Chevy the most, though. It had a blue and gray multicolored paint job, 22" inch rims. I only put 22s on it because I kept it rollin' up and down the highways, plus bigger rims and driving long distances on the highways ain't good. My interior was plush, butter-soft steel blue and gray seats, woodgrain everywhere, with four 12" inch TVs in the headrests. Two of 'em had built-in DVD players, an 8-inch in-dash touch screen radio that held 6 CDs or DVDs at once, and a 26" flip-down screen that the PlayStation was connected to, 18 speakers in total with four of 'em being 15" subwoofers that were neatly hidden behind the bench seat in the back that slid out to a bed at the touch of a button. You can tell I love that van from the way I just described it to you. If you haven't noticed, I didn't go into that much detail with any of my other whips.

The description of the van has nothin' to do with the story. I just wanted you to know that it was what I was runnin' up down the highway in all that day after leaving my uncle Doc's crib. My phones were going crazy, niggahs had drained me out of damn near every piece of dope I had by like 4 o'clock, almost everything. Remembering that RG and Shawn had told me that my niggah Bo had wurk, I texted him and told him I was on my way to see him. I was about two blocks away when he hit me back tellin' me it was cool fo' me to come through.

When I entered Bo's trap spot, I found damn near the whole 29th Street hood there, muthafuckas were everywhere just waiting around. I weaved my way from one room to the next where niggahs were deep in a dice game. I think they were playin' Fo' Five Six, I'm not sure though, so don't quote me on that. All I know is that the game was being shot on a nice size Pool table that was almost covered with money from the players placin' bets. A bunch of other guys, some I didn't know, were standin' around talkin' and matching blunts.

I made my way on through the two-way swinging door that led into the kitchen. Man, before the doors had closed behind me, good Bo's two big ugly mean ass red nose Pitbulls leaped up growling at me.

"Bro, if you love them muthafuckas, you better get 'em!" I said to Bo with my hand on my gun, ready fo' one of the monsters to come at me. Bo saw that it was me and silenced his two killas.

"Chill! Sit down!" he barked at the dogs and they instantly obeyed but kept an eye on me. I don't know why they don't like me. I ain't ever did shit to 'em. "AR, man, I need you to get on that stove and whip three of them keys up to one-fifty for me right quick, while me JR work on gettin' this here together!" he said as him and the homie JR stood at one of the two round glass tables that was in the kitchen, straining heroin through sifers.

"Damn, it seem like every time I come around you try to put me to work," I complained, as I got started busting down one of the bricks of cocaine into a large pot. "I got you though but I want a discount on what I need for providing my talent," I said as I added the soda and hot water.

"Bro, you know I got you. Fo' the rest of them niggahs in there I ain't givin' out no plays on shit. This shit crazy right now."

"AR, look at how you doin' that. You the only niggah in this bitch who can whip a whole thang at once like you doin' and it come out right right. That's why big bro be puttin' yo ass to work!" JR said, glancing over at me going to work at the stove.

"Whudeva, J. Y'all just scary!" I joked, then said, "Shid, Bo, I ain't worried 'bout them, I'm only worried 'bout me right now," I honestly replied while whippin' the contents in the hot pot up into a paste with a blender. As I did, it hit me that it had been a very long time since I'd seen Bo actually gettin' his hands dirty the way he was. I knew that times was about to get real hard fo' me when at the end all he could afford to sell me was a brick and a half soft. Most of that was gone befo' I decided to call it a night at 11:00 p.m. I was so tired from stress that I went over to Georgia's crib just to chill with her and fell straight to sleep on her couch. I didn't wake up until she was leaving for work the next day.

After promising to make it up to her, I let her go on to work and I went home and got right in the bed. I had every intention on sleepin' until sleep wouldn't let me sleep nomo'. That only lasted a lil' more than two hours. That's when uncle Doc called me and told me he needed me to come home to him immediately. From the sound of his voice I knew whatever it was was seriously serious. I made sure to grab my extra extended clip in case the ten rounds in my Glock wasn't enough to handle what he so urgently needed me for.

Chapter 22

Okay, so here's what happened with Unc. He'd been up earlier than usual feelin' mixed emotions of worry and anger because Fetty hadn't returned home. No, it wasn't unusual for her or any of his other girls to spend nights out at a time; it comes with their occupations. But it is unusual for Doc not to receive a call or text from any of them checkin' in with 'im. The girls checked in with him so much that they would text him just to let 'im know that they were in the bathroom or sittin' out on his front porch. So not hearing from Fetty had my uncle feelin' some typa way.

Normally, he would've just tracked her cellphone when he wanted to know who she was dealin' with without letting the trick that she's with know that he's there. But his three-year old had thrown Fetty's phone out the window and broke it and he had never set up the GPS on her new phone because of all of the excitement that came along when Shawn parked that U-Haul in his driveway. When Unc was in a bad mood, everyone in the house was in a bad mood, and bad moods aren't good for business. So, to keep everyone calm in the house, he took Billy—their little black and white pug—for a morning walk. The lil' dog was well trained, so Doc didn't walk him on a leash. Billy would never wander more than a few feet in front of him. The only time that the dog won't immediately obey Doc is when its playin' with one of the kids or one of the girls. But that morning, when they'd gotten like two blocks away from the house, the dog all of a sudden stopped then took off runnin' down an alley. Unc went chasin' after him.

When he'd caught up the whimpering dog, he also found Fetty lying dead in the bushes. The first thing Doc did was put the dog on a leash to keep it away from her, then called me. When I made it there, Unc could barely talk from finding Fetty dead. All I understood was when he pointed me towards the bushes. I went to check out what had him so shook up and that's when I saw her. From the way her eyes were and the color of her skin, I knew that she was dead. I didn't go any closer to the body. I just called the police and waited with my uncle on the other side of the filthy alley until they got there.

After answering questions and giving our statements to the female detective that my uncle knew— named Tony Lont—we were allowed to leave. I stayed over Doc's house for pretty much the whole day, because the man was so traumatized by findin' the young girl that he'd grown to love as his family lying like trash in the bushes. He was so much so that two hours after we got back to his house, he went outside and started choppin down all of the shrubbery that lined the front of his place. I could imagine how he was feelin' so I didn't even attempt to stop him. I just let him work it all out.

While we were mourning the loss of Fetty, King Tivon was down in Chicago getting himself prepared to put on a concert like he hadn't just murdered an innocent girl for nothing seventy-two hours before. I felt bad because I knew her, but I wasn't fucked up about it. The only reason I went to the funeral was to make sure that Fetty's family didn't try to get dumb with my uncle. He wasn't the one who made her into the whore and hustler that she was. They did. All my uncle did was put a roof over her head and did his best to protect her.

Like I said, I spent most of that day over by my uncle's. While I was there dealing with all of that, it was delivery day at the pharmacy where Georgia works and she was plotting to make her move. At lunch time her coworker had to make a personal run and wasn't sure if she would be back by the time her break was over with, so she asked Georgia to cover for her and clock her back in at the end of their lunch break. The coworker's timing couldn't have been more perfect. Georgia quickly agreed, accepting the magic key card from her airhead coworker, who Georgia knew was only leavin' work to run up behind her pure crackhead boyfriend.

As soon as he coworker had left the job, Georgia cut her own break short and made her way to the pharmacy's storage area. She swiped the coworker's security key card through the slot beside the heavy security door and when it opened she went inside. She found the place where the drugs were stored, then used the card again to open the cabinet and removed all of the extra bottles that she'd ordered fo' me. She placed them in a black garbage bag, locked the cabinet back up, then used the card to open the exit door that led to the big green dumpsters outside. Not wanting to have to climb inside of the dumpster to retrieve the bag of goods at the end of the day, Georgia smartly stashed the bag behind the dumpster and returned to work.

Back at her coworker's desk she logged on to her computer and manipulated the delivery inventory record to show the correct amount of pills that was in inventory, then sat back smiling, feeling slightly turned on by what she'd done. A few hours later, Georgia—when she'd gotten off of work—collected the goods and was heading home with the bag of prescription drugs sittin' on the passenger seat beside her when she received my text about what happened and askin' her did she like Chinese food.

I met up with Georgia in her parking lot. When we got in the house, she dumped the bag of drugs on the sofa where I was seated placing cartons of Chinese food out on the table for us. Seeing the large amount of stuff that she'd gotten made me as excited as her super freaky ass. I'll let you imagine what happened next. Just know a half hour or so later, we were sitting on the floor, Slim Jim ass naked, eating cold Shrimp Fried Rice.

Chapter 23

You know that saying "When it rains, it pours"? I never really believed in that saying 'til I found myself deep in a storm from hell, runnin' for shelter with a blindfold on. I'm tellin' you, after Fetty's murder things got crazy. All kinda things started happening at once.

Remember the magazine photoshoot that Tyneil done? Well, they were throwing a magazine release bash down in Chicago and it was a must that she attend. Tyneil didn't want to go alone, so while her and my sister were out getting their fingers and toes done she asked sis to attend the bash with her.

"Lexi, I've got to go to this magazine release party and I want you to come with me. It's the magazine that I'm going to have the centerfold in, so I gotta go and it'll be nice to have my favorite cousin to enjoy it with."

"I don't know, Ty," sis said with her mind locked on the location of the event. She knew King Tivon spends a lot of time in Chicago and feared that she might run into him. "I don't know if I'm ready to be going out of town by myself yet."

"You're not going to be by yourself. You're gonna be with me and I know there will be plenty of security there. Gurl, you can't let that punk ass nigga have you living in fear. You need to get out and enjoy your life like I'm sure he's enjoying his. Say you will go with me tonight please?" she begged. "Lexi, before you fix yo' lips to say no again just think, everybody who's a somebody is going to be up in there and you can do you some networking that'll help you get back to doing what you love. I know you miss that, so say yes."

"The only way I'll go is if my brother goes with us."

"Bitch, you know I don't mind if his fine ass come. I know he will come with us if you ask him the right way. Don't be on the phone soundin' all like you don't wanna go. If AR knows you really wanna, he'll make time for his baby sister, and maybe with a few drinks in him he'll give me a little of his time!" Tyneil said, smiling mischievously.

Just befo' I received the call from sis inviting me to go with them, I'd been on the phone with Flocko, my plug down in Chicago who'd been missin' in action lately. So, since I was going down there to hook up with him, I agreed to go to the party with her. My plan was to have RG ride down there with us but his girl decided that it would be a good time fo' her to give birth to his baby or since the lil' big head boy came early, maybe the baby felt it was time to introduce himself to the world. Either way you look at it, RG couldn't come with me. I thought about taking Shawn but he was busy tryna keep his trap house in order. So I said fuck it, I can go alone. I'd been fuckin' with Flocko ever since I met him in the Feds.

Until then I spent the day runnin' around collecting as much money as I could to put in Flocko's hands when we met, and the pills were right on time to make that happen. The pill money was 100% pure profit since I didn't really have to lay nothin' fo' them. Yeah, I planned to give Georgia somethin' like I promised her but I didn't have to give it to her right away, so I was good.

Just befo' entering the town of Sparta, I made a right turn on to a long gravel driveway lined with bushes and trees. I took it all of the way down and just like I was instructed. At the end I came to a double-wide trailer home sitting on a permanent cinder block foundation. I saw a lot of cars and

Pickup trucks parked every which way out in a field beside the trailer. I parked my Crown Vic right in front because I knew I wouldn't be stayin' there long. I was only up north to make a few deliveries; and because I promised my sister I'd go to the magazine bash with her, I didn't have time to waste. I still had to get home and get dressed.

I got out and followed the sound of the hard rock group, *Disturbed*, that was being blasted in the back of the place. Back there, I saw a bunch of drunk White folks partying it up. It was a crowd around a makeshift ring watchin' two dudes bare-knuckle boxing. Not seeing who I was there to meet in the crowd, I backtracked and walked up the stairs to the front door of the trailer. Befo' I could knock, a solid built huge 300-pound shirtless white boy appeared. He was covered in tattoos, one being a large black swastika in the middle of his chest.

"I knew I was going to have me some fun today," he grumbled, crackin' his fat fists, grinning at me mischievously.

"I like to have fun. I think everybody likes to have fun!" I replied, backin' back down the steps as he marched out of the trailer. As soon as my feet were on the ground, I drew my Glock and said, "But I didn't come up here to play. So if you don't want me to use that swastika fo' target practice then I think you should just go tell Bambi that AR-40 is out here for her."

"40! Put that gun away before somebody see it and all hell breaks loose!" Bambi said, comin' up behind me. I stepped to the side and glanced at the Kelly Clarkson lookin' chick but didn't lower my gun until she told the big boy that I was the person that she told him that she was waitin' for and to go in the backyard with the others until she and I were done takin' care of business. "Sorry 'bout my brother. He's been drinking, but he's a teddy bear at heart."

"A big racist teddy bear," I mumbled, puttin' my gun away. "Bam, I know you told 'im I was Black, so he was just on some pure bullshit just then," I said, walking back to my car.

"Wait. 40, please don't leave, honey," she pleaded, following beside me.

"Let's sit in my car and handle this, because I don't feel comfortable anyplace else over here," I admitted, noticing the group of white boys staring me down from the back of the trailer with Bambi's brother in their mix.

"Okay. Whatever you want, just don't leave. Let me run inside, honey, and get the money for you. Please don't leave!"

"They don't scare me," I lied. I was nervous as fuck but I wasn't gonna miss gettin' that money. "I ain't thinkin' 'bout 'em, so go 'head, I'm good!" I said, gettin' in the car and placing the burner on my lap for easy access, just in case the boys got tired of playing with each other in the backyard and came up front to really have fun. When Bambi came back she handed me the 5 geez that she told me that she for me and promised that she'll have another, plus a lil extra fo' my trouble when I came back. Just as I'd agreed, I gave her 2 Ziploc baggies of pills; one she paid upfront for, and the other she owed me for. I was gonna give her a third baggie but I was mad that she had me out there like that. "Bam, when I come back let's meet in town at a motel."

"Okay, honey," she agreed, then got out and ran in the house.

I pulled right off, kickin' up gravel, hoping to crack a windshield or two on their trucks and bikes. I looped my way into the town and gave my brother—Lil T—my last four and a split of soft to hold him over until I got back and collected 24 of the 28 geez that he needed for the brick he wanted. Not wanting to ride back home dirty, I fronted our guy—Coco—the other baggie of pills to sell. So I knew I had like 12 geez waiting fo' me when came back up there.

I got on the highway on ramp and received a text from Shawn askin' was I good. I hit him back and told him not until morning because I had an event to go to and it wouldn't be over until late. Then I cranked the volume on the radio and jetted back to the Mil.

Chapter 24

Shawn stared out the window at two cars of their crackheads that they'd just had to turn away, and he shook his head. It hurt him to have to turn away so much money but he couldn't do anything else at the time.

"What he say? Is he good or what?" Tone inquired when he returned from the door.

"Nah, he said he got some event to go to so it won't be until morning."

"Damn. What about yo' other guy RG, did you hit him?"

"Nope, but I doubt if he straight because him and AR are partners, plus he hit me up earlier and said that he was gonna be offline because his girl had just had a baby and had to be kept in the hospital fo' some shit!" Shawn explained as the doorbell rang for the hundredth time in an hour.

"Man, I know you know somebody else. We need to get some double ups or somethin'," Tone stressed as he went to answer the door. "Bro, the next muthafucka come to this damn house I'ma sell 'em some drywall," he said with a straight face.

"I knew somebody else who might have some wurk but I only met him once with RG but I've seen AR fuckin' with him a few times too. I think he might be one of their plugs, to tell you the truth."

"Call the niggah then. If he they plug, we should be able to get a better price from 'im and we won' have to go through AR nomo'."

"The thing 'bout him is I don't got that nigga Bo's number."

"Bo? you talkin' about Big Bo off 2-9?"

"Yeap, but his spot ain't over there though."

"I know some niggahs that rock with him. Let's ride down on 'im. I might see someone I know who can put us in with him. Niggahs don't turn down cash in their face." Tone was pushing Shawn because he'd spent most of his money on a BMW truck that he put in the paint shop right away and was now ready to be picked up. Only Tone didn't have the balance he needed without dippin' into their re-up money.

"Al'ight, I know somebody by his spot that get *loud*, and I need to smoke. So yeah, we can go on over there." Shawn agreed just to stop Tone from fuckin' up their trap by doin' something stupid like tryna sell the hypes drywall. Ten minutes later, they were parkin' in front of Bo's spot. At that same time, Shawn spotted his guy Albert, the person he was plannin' to get the weed from. He watched Albert enter the spot. "Aye, Tone, I just seen my niggah go up in the crib. I'ma call him and ask him to hook me up with Bo."

"Do yo thang," he encouraged while textin' on his phone. "Put it on speaker so I can hear what the niggah talkin'."

Shawn called Albert and set up the deal with 'im for an ounce of Kush, then asked him to let him holla at Bo.

"Wud it do, if it isn't Mr. Big Man himself. What can I do fo' you?" Bo said when he got on the phone.

"Wuss good, big bro! This Shawn, AR's guy."

"I know who you is, lil' niggah. Wuddup though?"

"I'm tryna get down and bust a move with you that ain't fo' this phone."

"Say less. I know you fuck with that white bitch, give me twenty minutes an' I can take you on 63rd Street. Fuckin' with her though gon' cost you another five hundred fo' the trip today if you really tryna fuck with me?"

"I'll be ready in twenty." Shawn agreed, then ended the call.

"Damn, I thought that niggah would be more playa than that. The bitch ass niggah taxin' us!" Tone complained about the extra $500 that Bo wanted for the wurk.

"Yeah, but it's soft and I know I can get Doc to whip it until it's almost double so when you think about it we winning," Shawn explained but didn't tell him that the tax was still less than what they would've gotten it from me for. But Tone was too upset by the number to understand what Shawn had just explained to 'im. All that was on Tone's mind was gettin' the money to get his ride out of the paint shop so he can get out flossin' in traffic in it. He was too in his feelings to know that with the deal that Shawn had just made had left 'im with the money he needed to do what he wanted to do.

"My niggah, I know this niggah be sellin' heroin too, so all these niggas that's runnin' in and out might be copin' from him. They all can't be hypes."

"Yeah, I guess."

"Yeah, so follow that nigga right there." Tone pointed to JR who was getting in his Audi A6. "I'ma stick that fool fo' his re-up and whudeva else he got and save us a few bucks. I'm sure yo' guy Doc know a muthafucka that'll take that H off our hands in one wop 'cause I don't wanna fuck with that shit."

"Tone, man, I don't know if you should—"

"Niggah, just follow him! I ain't tryna hear that soft ass shit. I got this!" he barked, greedily rubbing his palms together with his eyes glued to JR's car. Shawn followed the Audi across the city and on to the South side where it pulled over and parked. "Pull up in front of 'im. Park in front of that car right there!" Tone instructed.

"Man, I don't think you should fuck with dude," Shawn said, shakin' with fear. He'd never been a part of a robbery befo', so he was nervous as hell.

"Just wait here and keep the car runnin'." When Tone got out, Shawn briefly thought about pullin' off and leaving him to do the robbery on his own but he knew that he would have to deal with Tone later when he caught up with him, so he abandoned the idea. He watched Tone creep towards JR who'd just gotten outta his car and was slowly walkin' towards his house while chattin' on the phone. By the time JR noticed Tone and realized what was going on, it was too late. Tone snatched him around and shoved him to the ground. "Where that shit at, niggah? Make this hard if you want too!" he barked, holdin' his gun in JR's face.

"Don't shoot! You can have this shit!" JR told him instantly fumbling in his pocket and handin' Tone a large bankroll. "Here, take it."

"I want it all, bitch ass niggah. Don't try an' play me. Gimmie that dope too, niggah!" When JR insisted that the money was all that he had on him, Tone started viciously slappin' him with the gun. Then realized that JR had seen his face and pulled the trigger, shooting him twice in the chest. Tone ran his ass straight back to the car and Shawn sped off but not befo' JR's wife was able to take a picture of the Cadillac as it disappeared down the street.

Chapter 25

Once in the waiting room of the hospital, JR's wife—Christina—called her brother, Coop, and told him what happened to his best friend. At that very same moment that Coop was on the phone with her, Shawn was standin' right beside him actually paying Bo and Albert fo' the wurk and weed that he'd requested with the money that Tone had taken off of JR befo' leavin' their friend lying on the ground fightin' for his life. By the time she got around to sending Coop the photo of the car that she'd seen the shooter get into, Shawn and Tone were long gone.

Coop showed the photo to the others and they immediately recognized it as being mine. None of 'em were aware that I'd in fact sold the Caddy to Shawn almost a month before, but knowin' that there had to be more to it, Bo tried callin' me only to be told that the number had been disconnected. With my number all of a sudden becomin' out of service, Coop judged me to be guilty and put a hit out on me and whoever is caught in the car.

As you know, I wasn't even in the city when any of this happened. I was completely and totally in the dark. The reason the number that they had for me was out of service was 'cause I'd changed it that same day that we found Fetty's body, because my number is in the phone that the police had recovered off of her body. I changed the number for fear of it being tapped by the police. That's it, that's all. Bo had also tried to call RG whose phone was off because he was at the hospital watchin' over his newborn son. That's why I say I was runnin' for shelter with a blindfold on.

It was good and dark by the time I made it back to the Mil. I had a few things to do, so I had my sister help me while I showered and dressed. Tyneil had made it to sis crib just as she'd finished counting and banding the $165,000 plus that I'd collected for my meeting with Flocko. We road together in Tyneil's car because I didn't have time to switch out of my Crown Vic and I didn't think it would fit in well at the event. I was so wrong. The magazine release bash wasn't as bougie as I'd thought it would be. Some of everyone was there. Right through the door I ran into my niggah 2-4 Tank, who'd seen me at the same time I spotted him.

"Big bro, I didn't expect to see you up in here!" he said when he made it over to us.

"Shh, I ain't expect to see yo' ass here either," I replied shakin' his hand. "I see you takin' it to a new level."

"At the end of the day that's why we do what we do, right? A niggah caught a blessin' when my bitches got put in this magazine. I'm not tryna let it stop there though. I'm in here networking tryna keep some of that legit paper flowin'. I already got 'em booked in a couple of music videos shoots."

"That's wussup! Elevate, elevate, elevate. We need to sit down on a later date and see what we can put together that I can put a lil' bread behind!" I said, encouraging him and letting 'im know that I got his back at the same time.

While we chopped it up, I kept my eye on sis and Tyneil. I was surprised by how many people Alexis and Tyneil knew in the industry. They were being treated like royalty as they did some networking of their own. I had a few people inquire about my occupation, where I gave them the short version by replying that I do auto customizing.

It felt good to see my sister really happy, especially when the DJ asked her to join him in the booth. Lexi went up there and showed her ass with her mixing skills. She had the all way up. It was lookin' more like a night club in that bitch than a magazine release party. Alexis only blessed us with her talent fo' a lil over an hour before she relinquished control back to the house DJ. Not long after that, her and Tyneil was tellin' me that they wanted to leave because they'd found out that King Tivon is the person doing the special performance.

"That nigga man! Al'ight, let me tell Tank I'm gettin' outta."

"Go ahead—we'll be in the car," Tyneil said, then walked out with sis and one of the security guys.

I told Tank to get at me and was right out the door behind them. What we didn't know was that KT was already there watching us. He'd spotted Tyneil first, then Alexis when she was called up by the DJ. When KT was about to approach her, that's when her and Tyneil walked over to me. His first mind was to run up on me since now he was strapped and with his loyal entourage. But he knew if he did anything to me, especially in front of my sister, his chances of gettin' her back was dead. As if they weren't already after he raped her. The crazy man wasn't trippin' all that much 'cause seeing us all together told him that Alexis was hiding out in Milwaukee and he figured that Tyneil would lead him to her whereabouts real soon.

Our leaving the event early turned out to be right on time. As soon as we got in the car, I received the text that I'd been waiting for from Flocko. He asked me to meet him at a South side Chicago motel. To be safe, I left the money in the car and told my sister that I'll call her to bring it to me when I'm ready. Then I went and knocked on the door. I saw somebody peek out of the window before another person opened the door.

"Wussup, homie! I'm sorry about the time, but my people got this magazine thing going on and I had to be there to show support an' all that. You know how it goes."

"That's crazy. I just left it, the mag bash you talkin' about. The girl that was called up to DJ is my sister!" I said proudly, not thinkin' to mention that the centerfold is my family also. "We could've handled this way sooner had I seen you there."

"All you had to do was come over to the VIP area. I was right there the whole time!" he explained. "Let's get down to business so we can get back to it. I don't see anything in your hands. Should I assume you didn't bring the money with you or has my absence been that hard on my homie?"

"Both, to be honest!" I admitted, glancing at the duffel bag that one of the two Mexican goons that were securing the room with us was holding. "Homie, you can't be just vanishing on me like that, but I'ma hustla, homie, born and bred. I got some bread fo' you. I left it in the car with my sister. Let me text her an' tell her to bring it to me? It's just gonna be her. You know that I don't be on no foul shit."

Flocko agreed, and the standin' by the window playin' lookout did his job. Lexi came to the door and handed me the large *Coach* bag that she'd put the money in befo' we left the house, then hurried back to the car. "Let me see what you got good for me in the purse," Flocko said in a teasing tone.

"It's in ten thousand dollars' stacks to make it easy to count," I informed him, then emptied the bag out on the bed.

"AR, we're homies. We're good, I don't need to do that right now!" he said as he thumbed through a bundle of my cash before signaling his goon to hand me the bag of dope. "Leave me your bag to put this money back in. You can buy her another one with the extras I put in there for you. I can't have my homie out there bad now, can I?" We shook hands, then I left.

I drove us back home because Tyneil was a lil' tipsy, plus I'm the only one I trusted when transporting drugs across state lines. The whole trip back, I was thinkin' about how good things was going fo' me. I had my beautiful queen and a bitch on the side who wanted me bad. I had my sister in the back seat staring outta the window at the fading Windy City lights with a bag full of dope at her feet. I floated us down the highway in a comfortable silence all the way back to Brew City. When we pulled up to sis' crib, I expected Tyneil to spend the night but she said she had somewhere to be in the morning and took off. I didn't feel like goin' nowhere, so I stayed the night with sis.

    In the house I counted out twelve bricks that was in the bag. I'd only paid for eight. The four extra was a blessin' that was all mine. I shared the blessin' with RG by tossing 'im an extra one, givin' him three with the two that he paid for. I set aside two for Lil' T—the one he paid fo' plus another. I gave my niggah Carlos a whole one but he only paid up front fo' a half. Leaving me with the rest fo' myself. Since we didn't have nothin' else to do, me and sis went to work in the kitchen while we kicked it about everything. The wurk was so good that I could really do my dance with it. By the time we went to sleep, I was back to eight bricks. Ya know that's that dope boy magic.

Chapter 26

I got up early so I can get started running up and down the highways makin' my deliveries. Alexis offered to ride with me but I asked her to stay there to give RG, Carlos and Shawn what I'd left there for them. RG was the only one that I allowed her to let come to her house; nevertheless, I told her not to do anything 'til Tyneil got there with her. Tyneil arrived, followed by RG who stayed a while showin' off pictures of his newborn. This time Tyneil had led the crazy man to his heart's desire.

King Tivon was just about to get out of the car and knock on the door when he saw RG pull up and go inside. His anger and jealousy kicked up when he saw Lexi give RG a brotherly hug at the door when he came back out of her house. KT didn't see the hug as innocent. Right away, he went to thinkin' that RG was her new boyfriend. With his mind stuck on dummy, KT took off following my niggah. Every place that RG went was packed with our guys who he was droppin' wurk off to, so he couldn't get close enough to do anything to RG.

When RG did finally stopped in the perfect place, before he could get out to do anything, Coop and his guys had jumped out on RG an' commenced to beatin' his ass while demanding that he tell 'em where I was. KT didn't know what he was witnessing but he enjoyed watching the man he'd seen sis in the arms of gettin' beat bloody. In the end a MPD squad car that just so happened to be riding by pulled up on the men beatin' RG, some took off running but Coop and two others got caught and were placed under arrest. Witnessing that put King Tivon in such a good mood that he decided to take a different approach at tryna get Alexis back.

While the crazy man was plotting, I was headin' over to meet up with Lil' T up in Black River after dropping off a package to Chese in Appleton, which some of you don't know is on two different sides of the state. On my way to hook up with bro, I entered a storm, a bad one at that. I think it was a sign for me to stay away from that side of the state or somethin', but my motto is "*Get it in, and Get it gone*," so with the hard rain splatterin' down in a heavy continuous downpour I kept it movin'.

The funny thing is as soon as I made it to Lil' T, the rain had stopped. So maybe it was just cover fo' me to make it past Highway Patrol. Maybe it was tellin' me to slow down or even it's a sign lettin' me know if I don't give in and give up, that I would make it through the deadly storm that was brewing in my life. It's however one wants to look at it.

"Bro, your timing is perfect. I just got rid of the last five grams of what you left with me like two minutes before you pulled up an' I gotta couple of geez waitin' on a niggah right now!" bro told me when I got outta the car. I knew what he was tellin' me was the truth 'cause I'd seen a car pullin' away from him moments befo' I parked in front of him. "I hope this ain't like that last batch you gave me. I got it off but they talked shit about it."

"Hey, we had to work with what we could get at the time," I replied as we entered his crib. "Bro, this that flake here though. I got my real plug back on deck. Don't get too happy though 'cause the number is still the same. I can't drop the price just yet. It's still drought season."

"That's understood."

"But since we're family and all that, I brought you an extra one so together we can keep rising to the top!" I passed him the two bricks. "Just 'cause you got all of this don't mean you can start slackin'. I'm only able to do this fo' you 'cause my plug hit my hand for the wait!" I confessed. "The niggah expecting me to come back right an' I'm tryna go back with enough bread to make his ass make two trips to supply us."

"Fuck it, let's make his ass make three trips," Lil' T said, smiling as he was breakin' the wax seal on the brick.

"Ah, shit, I fo'got my phones in the car," I said more to myself than to him before joggin' back out to the car to get 'em. A text was waiting for me when I got my phones. A couple actually, one was from my BM tellin' me she had some vacation days comin' and wanted to know if I wanted to spend them with her or should she make other plans. I knew better than to tell her to make some other plans. Rhonda's askin' was her way of tellin' me what she wanted from me. My BM liked to travel the world on her vacation days and I didn't know if I could afford to be gone like that at the time, so I hit her back and told her we'll discuss it when I get back to the city later.

The other text made me smile. It was from my pill and powder girl, Bambi. She wanted me to bring her two ounces of powder. Walkin' back inside of the house with my brother in-law, I hit her back tellin' her I needed 3,600 plus 50 bucks fo' shippin' and handling. She hit back with the name and room number of a motel in town, just like I'd told her I wanted to do on my last visit. "Aye, aye, bro I'ma need two zips of that for the road. I gotta order fo' it just now."

"That's no problem. I'll just take it outta what I owe you." He was already weighing and packaging up the grams that he needed for the clients that he had waiting on him, so he quickly got to makin' up what I asked for.

I thought of Bambi's punk ass brother and decided to get me a lil' get back. So I jetted to Walmart and bought the vitamins that I needed to cut the dope up with and went to work turning forty grams into the fifty-six that she requested. Hey, the broad lucky I didn't go half and half on it fo' her havin' me around her racist ass people. Bro inquired about what I was doing because he'd never done anything with coke except cook it up.

"This works best when you know what the percent of your wurk is. Muthafuckas like to scream that hundred percent shit, but that's not ever true. No dope over here is hundred percent ever. This right here we got is a lil' over eighty-five percent, which is way better than that last batch which was on the high side of fifty percent. You gotta look for the flake and the rainbow in it. The deeper the rainbow is on the flake, the better it is. So even with me doing what I did, it's still better than that last shit we had!" I explained and he instantly got to work, finishing off the remainder of the vitamins.

Leavin' him to it, I got on my way to the motel down in Sparta. As I drove, I thought on Rhonda's upcoming vacation time. I was in my head makin' plans to take her and the kids to Wisconsin Dells for a weekend getaway. I'd been there before but never with my family, so her text had me feelin' like it was about time that I got on my family man an' let the thug shit rest fo' a while. People on the outside of the game lookin' in like to say that selling dope is easy money. Take it from a niggah that was born in a trap. Dope money is far from easy money. It's fast money, yes, but there's nothin' easy about putting in 20 to 24 hour shifts back-to-back. Or constantly lookin' over your shoulder for haters, robbers and the Feds.

Chapter 27

By the time I had my mind made up to go on vacation with the family, I'd made it to the motel and found the room which was located all the way on the end. Seeing that she'd chosen the perfect location to conduct business, I parked, got out an' knock on the door. I paid no attention to the big white Ford F-250 pickup truck that I'd passed when I entered the motel's lot. If I had been, I would've noticed the fat white boy sittin' in it had gotten on his phone as soon as he'd seen me. I also would have seen him when he got out and headed my way.

The door opened and I entered the room finding myself face to face with Bambi's brother who had a gun pointed at my head. I hadn't closed the door all of the way behind me yet so I instantly tried to dash back outta the room and ran smack dead into the fat boy from the truck. He shoved me back inside, walked in and closed the door behind us. I stood there with my hands up and my eyes on the gun now aimed at my chest, but showed no fear.

"Put everything you got on the table and I might not use your shirt for target practice," Big boy said, usin' my line on me. I shook my head mad at myself fo' being caught the way I was.

"Man, y'all sure do gotta weird idea of what fun is in this town," I grumbled as I placed the dope and money on the table. I only had a little more than a hundred bucks on me; the rest was stashed in the car with my gun.

"Where's the rest of the money?"

"That's all I got on me. I would have more if y'all were payin' me instead of robbing me." I put my hands down 'cause I could see that the clowns were on some dope fiend shit. "Look, dude, you got what you want. Now let me get the hell outta here so we'll never see each other like this again."

"Yeah, man, we got the stuff so let's get out of here," the fat boy behind me spoke up. "It's not like he can call the cops on us." He chuckled.

"I don't fuck with the police on no level. I ain't trippin' on that lil' shit there, it's all a part of the game. Man, my bitch just had a baby that I'm tryna go hold fo' the first time so just let me get outta here!" I lied, remembering the two infant footprints that I'd seen tatted on his shoulder, hoping that I could pull his heartstrings.

"It's not the cops that I'm worried about you telling," he said, walking over to me. "I don't want you talking to my sister." He passed his gun to his buddy, then immediately punched me in the chest, knockin' me backwards. I pretended that the blow had hurt me way more than it did. "Boy, now you're gonna feel my idea of fun."

He came at me fast, swinging hard. I covered up, catchin' most of his punches on my forearms and shoulders while watchin' the man with the gun the best I could. When I seen the fat boy lower the gun to his side that's when I started fightin' back. I punched big boy in the face, making him jump back in shock, then I spun around and attempted to kick fat boy in the nuts but hit all thigh meat. He punched me in the forehead and I fell to the floor. I immediately balled up and covered my head, ready fo' them to beat my ass. All they did was laugh and kick me a few times before they left the room.

You know that's where they fucked up at right? All they'd done was piss me the fuck off. Since they wanted to play city, I got on my thug shit fo'real fo'real. I didn't call my brother cryin' about what happened. I called Lil' T and told 'im that we had some gangsta shit to take care of and he was by my side in a flash. We concocted a plan and then we headed out to Bambi's trailer home in two separate cars.

When we arrived, the Ford F-250 was there and two other cars. The field was deserted, which told me that the only ones there were the people I could see through the windows movin' around inside the trailer. Bro took position at the back door with his gun ready and I went to the front door and kicked it in. All of the females inside screamed at the same time. I fired a shot into the wall behind them.

"Shut the fuck up!" I yelled at the same time as Lil' T had kicked his way in through the back door.

"40, please don't hurt me and my kids. I told them not to do it!" Bambi pleaded, hugging a young boy and a teenage girl close to her. I could see that Bambi's face was badly bruised and she had a fat lip that I assumed she'd received when she tried to talk her brother and boyfriend outta robbing me. Right or wrong, I gave her a pass.

"Bam, I believe you. Y'all good, I came here fo' them." I gestured with my gun. "Not you." I turned toward big boy who was sittin' in a chair staring me down. His face was burning red and he had a black eye from when I hit 'im in it at the motel. "I'm about to give y'all the fun you were lookin' fo'," I said, then went to beating the hell outta him with a brass lamp that I snatched off of the table. At the same time, bro was beating fat boy in the face with his gun in the kitchen.

Approximately fifteen minutes later, me and Lil' T were racing away from the trailer. He was headin' back up to Black River and I was on the highway headin' home. On my way, Alexis texted me and told me that RG needed me to call him asap. I did, wondering why he didn't just call me himself.

"Niggah, what the fuck did you do? You got niggahs jumpin' me looking for you! Get over here and tell me what the fuck is goin' on."

"Whoa, I ain't do shit. I'm not even there. Who jumped you and why they lookin fo' me?" I questioned, surprised by what I was told. At the time, the only thing I'd done was beat up them white boys for robbing me and I know he wasn't talkin' 'bout that because none of my clientele knew much about me.

"It was Coop, Snake an' a couple mo' of them 29th Street niggahs. So if you don't know what's going on then you better find out quick 'cause them fools at yo' head, bro."

"I'm finna call that niggah Coop right now."

"Him and Snake in jail. The police pulled up on 'em while they were kickin' my ass. I wonder if they think you had somethin' to do with what happened to JR."

"What happened to him?"

"Man, AR, you really don't know nothin' about nothin', do you? Somebody robbed and shot JR outside of his house. They don't think he gon' make it. I found out because I was in the same hospital he was at after them fools jumped me."

"I'ma call Bo. Fuck that, I'ma pull up on him as soon as I make it back down there."

"Niggah, why you ain't give me yo' new number?"

"I did when I called you so you could hook up with Lexi. Whudeva, this here my new number, save it. Watch yo'self, bro, 'cause I don't know what in the hell is going on fo'real. I doubt if it has anything to do with JR 'cause that's my niggah. I fuck with all of 'em over there the long way, so this shit crazy."

"I can't tell. You be on point 'til you get it straightened out. Love, bro."

"Love." I ended the call with my head all fucked up. Unable to wait, I called Bo and asked him what was goin' on. That's when he told me that JR got robbed and shot in front of his crib and his wife took a picture of my car speeding away. "What car?"

"Yo' Caddy. Who you got drivin' it 'cause I know this ain't you?"

"I sold that car to my lil' guy the other day. I really don't think he'd do no shit like that. Shawn ain't no robber."

"Shid, I just was fuckin' with Shawn, as a matter of fact he was by my spot when the shit happened so it couldn't have been him."

"Bro, I don't know what the fuck going on but Coop nem was foul fo' what they did to RG though. But I'ma ride down on you when I make it back down there so we can figure this shit out. Y'all know me. You should know I'd never be on nothin' like that."

"I told them fools that but they went on some in-their-feelings shit because you changed yo number all of a sudden!" Bo explained.

"This my new number we on right now. I changed it because the police got ahold of a phone with my old number in it and I ain't taken no chances on 'em tappin' my line." After explaining everything and makin' plans to hook up the following day, we got off the phone. I thought about callin' Shawn but wanted to be lookin' in his eyes when I asked him about what happen. I was already guessin' Tone's rogue ass had somethin' to do with it.

Chapter 28

When I made it to the crib, I dropped off the cash and swopped out guns, because the one I had was filthy from the beatin' I gave out with it. After that, I hooked right up with Shawn. He confirmed that Tone had robbed and shot JR. Shawn claimed that he didn't have nothin' t do with it and that he didn't know that Tone was going to shoot JR. I made him give me all of Tone's info and warned him not to tell him or anyone that we were lookin' fo' him. I also told him never to say that he was with Tone when it happened again because them 29th Street niggahs would kill him on the spot just fo' bein' guilty by association. As soon as I got Tone's info, including a photo of his new whip, I forwarded it to Bo and told him I'll holla at 'im when we can hook up.

Bo took the info and photo I'd provided him on the rogue and gave it to his two young, eager-to-please goons, Cash and Boom. He told 'em to make sure that he would have a close casket funeral, even though JR hadn't died from his injuries. With the kill order given, the two goons headed out and went in search of Tone. Boom was new to the hood so I didn't know too much about him, but Cash I do know and he's a plum fool. So for 'em to be so close as they are, Boom had to be just as foolish. Honestly, I didn't care, just as long as they was off my ass. But I kept my burner close just in case somebody didn't get the memo.

After the day I had, I took the rest of it off and headed straight to Rhonda's to chill and discuss the vacation plans.

After lookin' in on the kids, I made my way into her bedroom where Rhonda was once again standing in front of her vanity table. Only this time she was fully dressed in an emerald and gold Dior tracksuit that I could see hugged her ass just right. I watched her tease her hair with some type of oil sheen.

"I see you're going out someplace," I said, approaching her.

"I was invited out for drinks," she confessed, looking at me through the mirror as she finished her hair, then turn around holding a gold charm bracelet out to me. "Can you fasten this on for me?"

"Really—You want me to help you get all sexy fo' the next nigga?" I said, half joking while locking the bracelet on her wrist.

"Stop it. You don't hear me sayin' shit about you goin' out with them raggy ass hoes you be out with!" she retorted, smiling.

"I don't ask you to help me get dressed to go out with 'em either. But we ain't talking 'bout me!" I said, wrapping my arms around her and holdin' her close.

"I don't know if this jealousy act you're puttin' on right now is real or just play," she questioned, staring in my eyes.

"Just give me a kiss so I can go home an' pout alone in the dark." She kissed me, then pulled out of my arms. "Since you're going out, I take it that you don't gotta work tomorrow?"

"Nope, I'm off, yesss, yes! Why you ask?"

"No reason, just being nosey. Wantin' to know what my Luv has up, that's all. I did come over here to chill with you so we can talk about yo' vacation time. But since you got other plans, me and the kids will just go find us somethin' to get into."

"We can talk when I get back. The kids been bugging me about going skating. I'll be home by the time skating is over and we can talk then."

"Alright, skating it is and I'll see you when we get back." Once my BM was all done with her beautification process, I walked Rhonda out to her car, then went back in and got the kids. We went out to the roller skating rank in Butler. I'm almost always the only Dad alone there with his kids. Like always, my Princess takes time out to play *Deal Or No Deal* with me and help me eat the pizza that I always got stuck finishing it off. Man, I miss those times.

But anyways, later that night while laying together in bed, my BM told me that she wanted time away from the kids with just the two of us. I explained to her that I couldn't afford to really go anywhere the way she likes to do because of all of the nonsense that's going on.

"I don't care where we go just as long as you make it feel like a getaway," she said, lying in my arms.

That's all I needed to hear. The next day I call Lil' T because he has the type of connections that I needed to give Rhonda her special time. I asked him could he get me a cabin. He was able to make it happen fo' me, but only for a weekend. So, instead of wasting Rhonda's two-week vacation, I took her weekend off. I didn't tell her where we were going, just for her to pack a bag. I was waiting for her at the house when she made it home from work that Friday evening. I greeted her with a kiss, then told her to get her bag so we can get our kid-free, phone-free, romantic weekend started. She ran inside and was out with her bag befo' I could blink. We went in my Tahoe and took off.

After driving Northeast for a while, I turned onto a bumpy gravel road that was lined with trees and wild flowers. At the end, I stopped and parked in front of a cabin surrounded by woods and a lake off just behind it. Rhonda was all smiles when she stepped outta the truck. I grabbed our bags and led the way inside. The inside of the place was just as nice as the outside. I knew that I owed lil' bro big time for getting us that place. It was nothin' of what I expected. He had only sent me pictures of the outside, not the inside.

We walked hand in hand through the cabin, checkin' it out, finishing our self-tour out on the back deck, where we found a romantic view along with a Jacuzzi, fire pit and well-kept patio furniture.

"Do this feel like a getaway? Nope. Don't answer that yet. Go in there and get outta them work clothes and slip into somethin' sexy."

"What make you think I packed somethin' sexy?" she asked, grinning.

"If you didn't, your birthday suit will be sexy enough. As a matter of fact, I'ma get the Jacuzzi together for us while you're gone." I'd lit candles and had torches burning on the deck and sat out four chilled bottles of her favorite wines in the coolers.

When she came back outside fifteen minutes or so later, the sight of her had me on brick. She was wearing a sheer lace black teddy and no panties. I passed her a wild cherry flavored wine cooler, and led her over to the daybed where we began kissin' enveloped in the soulful sounds of Jagged Edge singing their hit song, *Promise*. As we continued kissing, our clothes came off; it felt good being outside completely naked in a moonlit darkness. Laying her down, I poured a little of my strawberry cooler on her breasts and slowly sucked and licked it off.

Not wanting me to have all of the fun, she rolled over on me and kissed her way down my body to my hardness and poured her cooler on it, then slowly and sensuously sucked it off. She didn't stop suckin' until she felt I was about to cum. Neither one of us were ready for that just yet. I flipped her back up under me an' started lickin' every inch of her blossom, dancin' my tongue around her clit before covering her body with mine, sliding my hard, swollen length into her wet warmth. Then, slowly and intensely, I made love to her as Jagged Edge went from singing *Promise*, to *Surface*, singing passionately. Presently, she began cumming for me over and over 'til I couldn't hold back any longer and filled her.

Chapter 29

While I was up north giving my BM a refresher on the language of love, Cash and Boom were standing in the dark about to commit murder. After searching and staking out all of the places that they knew to look for Tone, they finally spotted his BMW X6 pickin' up what they assumed to be a young prostitute on North Avenue. The goons followed until the truck had parked in the perfect isolated area for them to handle their business. Sick-minded, the two goons stood in the shadows watchin' their target put on a show that was a bit too energetic for him to doing with a prostitute, no matter how fine she is.

They watched as Tone pulled the girl out of her tube dress as she was undoing his jeans. Cash wanted to kill 'im when he was pullin' off his shirt over his head, but Boom stopped him because he wanted to watch Tone fuck the lil' bitch for a minute first. Yeah, the niggah Boom is a freak ass bastard, but then again why not let Tone get the last pussy that he'll ever get again befo' he dies? Tone slid towards the middle of the backseat and pulled her on top of him.

The two standing watch heard the girl start moaning loudly and smiled. When the windows of the truck started to fog up, Boom was ready to do the hit. They calmly ambled over to the BMW and stood lookin' through the window at 'em. The girl's back was to them so she couldn't see 'em but Tone could. When the goons' shadows caught Tone's eye, he looked over the girl's shoulder and right into the face of

Boom. Tone started to push the girl off of 'im, instinctively thinkin' he could get to his gun, but as soon as Boom noticed Tone spotting them he started shootin' into the truck. The hard impact of the slugs caused the girl to slam into Tone. He quickly used her as a shield, clutchin' the dead girl to his chest and screaming for the Lord.

Not being able to hit his target, Boom stopped firing and Cash ran around to the other side of the truck and snatched the door open, causin' Tone to fall half outta the doorway. Immediately, Tone started to beg fo' mercy. The only mercy he received from Cash was a quick death as the goon emptied his clip into his face, makin' sure that he'd done as he was ordered to do befo' the two of 'em stripped Tone's dead body of its cash and jewelry, then ran off into the night.

As much as we wanted to, we couldn't stay inside the cabin all weekend because we had to eat. Since Rhonda was not a fan of fishing, that next afternoon we took a trip up to La Crosse to get a late breakfast and decided to spend the day shoppin' and sightseeing. Surprisingly, it wasn't me who had to cut our weekend getaway short. Rhonda had checked her email and found that she been called into the hospital to work. Being suddenly called in to work was the down side of workin' in one of the largest hospitals in the US.

Well, with our trip cut short, I got us home and then got back on my grind. I was back on the highway by 5:00 o'clock that evening. I'd gotten a call from another one of my big pill and powder clients who wanted me to meet him at his place with three ounces soft, two hard and fifty pills. After what I'd gone through with Bambi on the other side of the state, you would think I would've had enough of dealin' with big dopefiend white dudes and trailers homes, but nope. Had to go get that cash and just 'cause Bambi's people were full of shit didn't mean everyone who lived in trailers were the same.

I told myself this as I waved my way through the trailer park and parked in front of the home that I was lookin' fo'. I got everything that Cowboy had ordered out of the stash and placed it on the floor of my car and put my gun in my waistband and went up to the door and pressed the doorbell. The female that answered the door did not look like she belonged in a trailer park or even messin' around with a big biker named Cowboy. She easily put me in the mind of the actress Scarlett Johansson.

"Can I help you?" she inquired from behind the screen door.

"Is Cowboy here?" I'd leaned against the banister while waitin' for her to answer the door; when I did, my shirt had tightened, showin' the handle of my gun. I wasn't aware of it until she raised the gun that she'd been hidin' off to the side of the door.

"Whoa, lady, chill. Cowboy knows me, tell 'im AR out here."

"He's not here yet but they're on their way," she said, makin' sure to emphasized the *they*. "Cowboy don't like me letting in people and I don't want to shoot you but I will if you try anything."

"It ain't no need fo' all that. I'm not on nothin'. I'll wait in my car if that's alright?"

"I'll feel better if you put the gun you got under your shirt inside the mailbox so I can keep an eye on it."

"That's not gonna happen. What I'll do fo' you though is . . . I'll put it in my trunk so I don't forget it and sit in my car where you can see me while I wait?" She agreed and I put that gun in the trunk like I said I would, then got in the car and grabbed my other one from beneath the seat and bumped Lil Boosie's song—*Better Not Fight*—while I waited.

Chapter 30

While I was sittin' up in a trailer park wondering what's wrong with people, King Tivon was pullin' up to sis' house. He sat mumbling to himself what he'd plan to say to her while watching her place for a while befo' gettin' out. He strolled onto the porch and rang the doorbell. Lexi had just finished a call with her mother when she heard the doorbell. She grabbed her purse thinkin' it was the food that she ordered. When she peeked through the peephole and saw the source of her nightmares, her purse slipped from her hands and she instantly ran and grabbed the gun I'd left there with her.

"Oh my God! Get away from my house!" she yelled through the door when she returned with the gun and her eyes filled with tears of fear.

"Babe, I just want to talk to you. I need to apologize to you. Please Lexi, baby, let's just talk?"

"No! No! I—don't ever wanna talk to you again. Get the hell away from my house. I called the police!" she lied, knowin' calling them wouldn't be a good idea with the large amount of drugs in the house. Alexis gripped the gun the way Rhonda had taught her and peeked through the blinds of the window, ready to bust it if he hit that door.

"Okay, I'ma go. I'm going to leave this I got for you outside the door. Lexi, if you're not ready to talk to me in person, would you please let me call?" he inquired. When she didn't answer, he set the flowers and gift bag down, then jogged back to his truck and pulled right off.

Sis was trembling from the fear and adrenaline. She watched the truck 'til she couldn't see it nomo', then dropped to her knees cryin'. She sat there until she cleared her head enough to move again. That's when she got her phone and called me.

"Wuddup, sis?"

"He found me! I don't know how but he found me! The bitch came to my house!" she told me, sobbing in the phone.

"I'm on my way. Don't go nowhere and don't open the door. I'm on my way. I'm on my way right now."

"I won't. I-I got the gun."

"Good, keep it with you but don't go nowhere. I need to get off the phone befo' I have an accident on this freeway!" I said, doing 90mph through the evening traffic.

When we got off of the phone, Alexis called Tyneil who didn't answer, then she called Rhonda. My BM told her that she was on her way and instructed her not to leave the house just as I had. Sis told her that she was scared, so she told her to lock herself in the garage in case he do come back and break in befo' we got there. That's exactly what Lexi did.

Rhonda had to get off the phone with her so she could tell her supervisor that she had an emergency and had to go home. With or without his permission, she was leavin' to go be with my sister.

It was kinda drizzling rain when I skid to a stop in front of my sister's crib. I ran up on the porch with my gun in hand and found the flowers and gift bag. I picked it up and used my key to let myself inside. I called Alexis at the same time my foot kicked her purse that was spilled out on the floor. I dropped the bag, runnin' through the house, yelling her name, callin' her phone and lookin' everywhere. She wasn't there and she wasn't answering the phone. When I ran back outside, my BM was just comin' up the steps with her gun at the ready because she'd seen the front door wide open like I left it.

"Rhonda, do you got Lexi with you 'cause she ain't in here an' she ain't answering her fuckin' phone?"

"No. She not answering for me neither. Let's check the garage. She told me that she was scared to be in the house alone so I told her to go lock herself in her car in the garage and wait for me!" Rhonda explained, then we rushed to the garage in back of the house.

I tried the latch; it was locked. I called her name and banged on the door. Rhonda ran over to the window and saw her truck was still in there but she couldn't see if Alexis was inside 'cause it was dark in the garage and her windows were tinted. I stopped banging and listened, I heard a low humming sound like the truck was runnin'. I banged on the door again then said fuck it, stepped back and kicked the door open and rushed inside with my BM right behind me.

"Lexi—Alexis!" We both yelled, poundin' on the truck's windows, thinkin' she'd fallen asleep. When she didn't respond, the panic that I was already feeling increased. I pushed Rhonda out of the way and broke out the driver's side back window with my gun. I had to hit it like three or four times befo' the damn glass shattered. When it did, I reached in and hit the *unlock* button on the door; as soon as it popped, Rhonda snatched the door open and tried to wake her up. But even with her shaking her, sis wouldn't come to. She wouldn't respond. Soon, the carbon monoxide from the truck running in the closed garage was starting to mess with our breathing.

"We need to get her outside now!" Rhonda ordered me, and started pullin' Lexi outta the seat.

I came over and scooped her up and carried her out of the garage into the fresh air. I put her on the ground like Rhonda told me too. She only let my sister lay motionless on the wet ground for a few heavy moments to see if she would come to. When nothing changed, Rhonda went to work giving her mouth-to-mouth.

"Breathe, sis, breathe!" I pleaded, kneelin' on the other side of them.

"Breathe, Lexi. Come on, gurl, breathe!" Rhonda exclaimed, pumping sis' chest a few times before giving her mouth-to-mouth again.

"Don't do this to me, Lexi. Breathe for us—please, God, make her breath." I prayed at the same time dialing 9-1-1. "They want to know if she has a heartbeat."

"Tell 'em yeah but it's weak. Tell 'em I'ma nurse and I'm going to continue doing chest compressions until they get here!" Rhonda replied, then listened to the beat of Alexis heart again befo' going back to work on her. She gave her mouth-to-mouth one mo' time before finally gettin' sis to start breathing on her own. "She's back!" she shouted as she wiped rain outta her eyes. "Come on, gurl, you can do it!" my BM encouraged her, watchin' as Alexis's chest started rising and fallin' with a regular strength of her own.

"That's it, Lexi. Keep breathin' for me. Keep breathin'," I mumbled, half holding my own breath as I stood watch. I didn't remember to breathe my damn self 'til I heard her start moanin' and tryna get up.

"No, no, Lexi. Lay down, just lay still and breathe. We're here—we here. I got you!" Rhonda told her, wiping away rain and tears of joy.

I was fightin' back tears of my own, I can't lie. But as soon as the EMTs got there to take sis to the hospital, my anger returned. I told Rhonda to ride to the hospital with her and I stayed in the house sittin' in the dark prayin' that KT brought his crazy ass back. I was tired of his shit. It was the third time that I know of that the niggah had hurt my lil' sister and this time she could've died. I was so mad that I sat thinkin' of ways that I wanted to torture and kill 'im.

Chapter 31

While I was sittin' in the dark house plotting a murder, the night turned to day. It was light outside by the time I got the call to go pick Rhonda and sis up from the hospital. I brought 'em back to sis' house. Alexis didn't wanna be there but I told her that she was safe there and that I was going to put an end to everything once and fo' all. My BM knew I meant my every word because I hadn't called none of my guys over. She reluctantly went home to the kids, promising that she would be back to check on sis after she got herself rested. I sent my sister to her bedroom to get some more rest after almost dying from carbon monoxide poisoning.

Almost an hour later, when I got up from my post in the chair in the living room, to use the bathroom, I peeked in on my sister and saw her layin' on her side balled up with her knees to her chest clutching the gun that I'd left there with her. My anger instantly spiked up some more and I went and eased the gun from her fingers. I knew that the only way to end the livin' nightmare that Lexi was livin' 'cause of King Tivon is with his death. I couldn't see it any other way where my sister would be happy and at peace without knowin' that the crazy man was lying cold in a hole covered in dirt.

Jus' befo' noon, Lexi and my BM were sittin' in the office of Detective Stark who's head of the Special Felonies Division in the Milwaukee Police Department, explaining everything that King Tivon had done to my sister.

"How did he find out that you were in Milwaukee?" Stark asked. Sis shrugged and told 'im that she don't know. "Do you have an idea where he could be staying?"

"I don't know anything about him other than what I already told you!" she responded, raising her voice. Detective Stark felt that Alexis might feel better talkin' to another female, so he when he spotted Detective Lont he stopped her and called her into the office.

"Tonya!" Stark shouted as his fellow detective was walking by. When Lont stopped, he introduced Alexis to the plain-clothes female detective and quickly briefed Lont on what the issue was befo' leavin' them to talk.

Detective Lont listened to every word that Lexi repeated to her while simultaneously looking King Tivon up on the computer. What Lont didn't know was that she was lookin' at the face of the muthafucka who's responsible fo' the unsolved homicide that she's working on. Lont told sis that she will have them patrol cars in her area keep an eye on her house and for her to get another restraining order.

"A restraining order won't stop him. I tried that before. I moved all of the way out here and that hasn't stopped him."

"Our hands are pretty much tied until he actually tries to hurt you again. Right now all I know is that he came to your home with flowers wanting to talk with you. There's no crime in that. I know how it sounds, and I believe you but my hands are tied at this point."

"That's crazy!" Rhonda snapped. "That could be the time that he takes her life and then what? Come on, Lexi, let's go!"

"I get it, I understand," Lont said in a heartfelt tone. "Don't go try taking the matter into your hands, ladies. It's not worth throwing your lives away over some piece of trash like him. It's not worth it."

"What life?" sis retorted. "I thought I was starting a new one by running to a new place. But it didn't work and I may have made things worse. I'll tell you this much—I'm tired of running." With that said, sis followed my BM outta the building.

When they made it back to the house, we all sat down brainstormin', tryna come up with a plan to get rid of Lexi's nightmare. That's when sis saw the gift bag that I'd brought in the house and remembered that KT had told her that his number was on the card. I instantly thought of what Bambi's people had done to me and knew it would work on KT. I instructed Lexi to call 'im and tell him that she would talk to him but only in a public place. She didn't wanna hear his voice so she texted 'im from a burner phone. I was doubtful that doing it by text would work but the crazy man responded within seconds, agreeing to her terms. I had her tell 'im to meet her at the George Webb's diner downtown just off of 3rd and Wisconsin Avenue. When he agreed, I instructed Alexis to go to Rhonda's crib with her until they heard from me.

We all left the house together, going our separate ways. I went to the hood to holla at Bo an' nem. That's when I found out that Tone had been dealt with. To be on the safe side, me and Bo went up to the hospital to visit JR who was awake and ready to go home. He confirmed that Tone was the one who'd shot him and told me he never once thought I was behind any part of it. With that said, I knew I was officially all good in the hood again. Had things went a different way, I was more than ready to end our over 20-year brotherhood.

After that, I rode down on Shawn, who was stressed the fuck out tryna work a trap house alone. I told him to find him some lil niggahs to work it fo' him. He had a couple of guys who bought 8 balls from him here and there come through while I was there. I hollered at 'em for him and they happily filled the open position. I had to instruct Shawn on how to do everything from setting up shifts to his payroll. The spot may as well have been mine.

Befo' I left 'im, I told him to get the Caddy painted asap so it won't kick up no old hard feelings that could get him killed. There was no need for us to have a conversation 'bout Tone. Shawn knew that when he couldn't reach Tone on the phone and when Lala had told him that her brother hadn't been home and she couldn't reach 'im, that he would be attending Tone's funeral soon. Yeah, it was sad, but the niggah Tone had always played the game foul, and fo' doing so he received what he had comin'. I didn't shed a tear for 'im.

Chapter 32

Leaving Shawn's spot had me in my head about my plan to deal with King Tivon. Knowing when something happens to someone's spouse, the police's number 1 suspect is the one remaining. Even though sis and the crazy man weren't married, the police would still come at her, especially since she went in and filed a report with 'em about 'im. Even though my sister loves me, I didn't t trust that she would hold up under that kinda pressure. Well, I shouldn't say that I didn't trust her 'cause that's like sayin' I don't trust her, and I do. I just wasn't sure and I didn't wanna take the chance to find out. So I modified the plan.

Man, I went to Family Dollar and bought a bunch of big block white candles, a box of baking soda, wax paper, and a box of latex gloves. Then I went to the crib and went to work melting down the candles. I removed the wicks from the melted wax befo' adding the bakin' soda and blending it thoroughly together. Leavin' the wax mixture on the stove, I lined a shoe box with wax paper, then poured the mixture in and placed it under a fan. Once it had hardened, I pulled on gloves and pulled it outta the box, peeling away the paper befo' droppin' it in a Ziploc bag and wrapping it in duct tape. The tape is so the fake kilo of crack looked the part.

I don't know what made me think of the mixture. I'd never seen it done befo' nor had I ever heard of anyone doing it. It just popped in my head and I went with it. I'm always thinkin' of things like that and how to make stuff better.

I guess it comes from all of them long lonely hours I've spent running up and down the highways. Who knows, one day one of my ideas might make me a rich man.

Anyways, to pull my plan all together, I called Georgia and asked her if I could use her car because mine were too flashy for the move I needed to make. She said yes like I knew she would. To make her happy, I swopped my Camaro with hers and gave her $2,500 from the pill sales. I could have used one of the cars that I had up for sale at the time but hers was tinted out and mine weren't. At no point did I plan on her car ever to be seen. I just needed somethin' low-key while I sat in the diner's parking lot and waited fo' KT's arrival, but as a precaution I flipped the car's plates upside down to make 'em harder to remember.

King Tivon arrived at the diner right on time, went right inside and waited. After about ten minutes or so, the burner phone started ringing; he was sending texts askin' Lexi where was she. When he didn't get a response, he tried to sweet-talk her into answering. I was in the car crackin' the fuck up, reading the lame ass texts that he was sendin'. I wanted to text back and fuck with his head so bad but I didn't want him to get mad and leave like that. For my plan to work, I needed him to take me back to where he stayin'. Almost an hour later, he gave up waiting and I watched him exit George Webb storming mad and get back in his truck.

That's when, pretending to be my sister, I sent 'im a text tellin' him that I didn't feel comfortable coming out to meet him at night and that maybe we could do it in the day time tomorrow and prayed he took the bait. He responded sayin' that she didn't have to be afraid of him and that he would never hurt her again, and all that bullshit. The only thing I cared to read was him agreeing to the meet the next day.

I placed the phone on silent an' dropped it in the cupholder as I followed the black Denali outta the parking lot. From the speed and reckless way KT was diving, I could tell the niggah was furious. I made sure to keep a nice distance behind 'im so that he didn't notice me following him. He led me all the way out by the airport to one of the cheapest motels on the strip. Me being a thug, his choice of motels told me a lot—especially knowin' the punk had millionaire status. Cheap motels like the one King Tivon was stayed in didn't ask questions. As long as you had the money to pay for the room, you didn't even have to even give 'em a name.

Out of habit I put the burner phone in my pocket. I had on a black pullover hoody with a zipper pouch in the front. That's where I put the phone and fake kilo after slippin' on a pair of dark blue workman's gloves that I'd taken along with a 4 maybe 5-inch heavy iron pipe from my garage when I picked up the Camaro. My plans for the pipe was to give the bitch boy all of the ass beatings that his daddy should've given 'im. You know I had my heat on me for after our understanding was met.

Anyway, I slid the pipe up my right sleeve and swiftly caught up to him. The location of his room was both good and bad. It was good 'cause it was the first room on the far end of the building at the top of the stairs. An' it was bad 'cause it was at the top of the stairs. That meant that after I murdered the bitch, I would have to run down the steps or jump from the second floor.

The crazy man was so into textin' on his phone, that he paid me no mind. I could've did 'im right there and there but like I said, I wanted to punish him first. As soon as he pushed his room door open, I dropped the pipe into my hand and whacked him on top of his head, crackin' his melon. He staggered inside of the room holdin' his head and in the same motion KT turned around to see who'd done it. With blood pouring down his face he threw his arm up, blockin' my next blow with his forearm. I heard the bone break when it connected. KT yelled out in pain, then suddenly rushed me, ramming his shoulder into my chest. I fell against the door slammin' it all of the way shut, but I sprang back up at him;

that's when he swept my feet from under me. I hit the floor on my ass. He got to kickin' me, going crazy or crazier. I managed to scuffle away from his attack and get back on my feet. King Tivon went to pick up the pipe that I'd dropped; that's when I drew my gun and ended the battle with one shot to the side of his head.

Knowin' that everybody in the motel had heard us fighting, they especially had heard the gunshot. I quickly took out the fake kilo and threw it on the bed, then I went in his pocket and took out his money and tossed it in the air lettin' it fall wherever it did. I also took his phone befo' fleeing the room. As soon as I opened the door, I saw the others guests of the motel all lookin' up at the room, so I leaped from the top floor and ran my ass off. I could hear approaching police cars as I sprinted away.

Once I'd made it around the motel next door to the one I'd ran from, I pulled off my gloves and hoody. I rolled the gloves up in the hoody the long way, then tied it around my waist, making sure it hid my gun. Then, as calmly as I could, I walked all of the way around the block and right back into the parking lot across from the scene of my crime, got in the car and went back to Georgia's crib.

After feeding her a story about me gettin' jumped and robbed, I got in my Camaro and went to my BM's house. I told her and sis that the bitch ass niggah won't be trouble ever again. Later on that night, while we were watching the movie, *Daddy's Home*, and eatin' ice cream and pizza with the kids, Rhonda received a Breaking News Report on her tablet with the headline reading: *Up and coming rapper found slain in motel room, drug related activity suspected.*

To be continued

Lock Down Publications and Ca$h Presents Assisted Publishing Packages

BASIC PACKAGE $499 Editing Cover Design Formatting	UPGRADED PACKAGE $800 Typing Editing Cover Design Formatting
ADVANCE PACKAGE $1,200 Typing Editing Cover Design Formatting Copyright registration Proofreading Upload book to Amazon	LDP SUPREME PACKAGE $1,500 Typing Editing Cover Design Formatting Copyright registration Proofreading Set up Amazon account Upload book to Amazon Advertise on LDP, Amazon and Facebook Page

***Other services available upon request.
Additional charges may apply

Lock Down Publications
P.O. Box 944
Stockbridge, GA 30281-9998
Phone: 470 303-9761

Submission Guideline

Submit the first three chapters of your completed manuscript to ldpsubmissions@gmail.com. In the subject line add **Your Book's Title**. The manuscript must be in a Word Doc file and sent as an attachment. Document should be in Times New Roman, double spaced, and in size 12 font. Also, provide your synopsis and full contact information. If sending multiple submissions, they must each be in a separate email.

Have a story but no way to send it electronically? You can still submit to LDP/Ca$h Presents. Send in the first three chapters, written or typed, of your completed manuscript to:

LDP: Submissions Dept
P.O. Box 944
Stockbridge, GA 30281-9998

DO NOT send original manuscript. Must be a duplicate.
Provide your synopsis and a cover letter containing your full contact information.

Thanks for considering LDP and Ca$h Presents.

NEW RELEASES

BLOODLINE OF A SAVAGE 1&2
THESE VICIOUS STREETS 1&2
RELENTLESS GOON
RELENTLESS GOON 2
BY PRINCE A. TAUHID

THE BUTTERFLY MAFIA 1-3
BY FUMIYA PAYNE

A THUG'S STREET PRINCESS 1&2
BY MEESHA

CITY OF SMOKE 2
BY MOLOTTI

STEPPERS 1,2&3
THE REAL BADDIES OF CHI-RAQ
BY KING RIO

THE LANE 1&2
BY KEN-KEN SPENCE

THUG OF SPADES 1&2
LOVE IN THE TRENCHES 2
CORNER BOYS
BY COREY ROBINSON

TIL DEATH 3
BY ARYANNA

THE BIRTH OF A GANGSTER 4
BY DELMONT PLAYER

PRODUCT OF THE STREETS 1&2
BY DEMOND "MONEY" ANDERSON

FO'EVA ROLLIN' | ASSA RAYMOND BAKER

NO TIME FOR ERROR
BY KEESE

MONEY HUNGRY DEMONS
BY TRANAY ADAMS

Coming Soon from Lock Down Publications/Ca$h Presents

IF YOU CROSS ME ONCE 6
ANGEL V
By Anthony Fields

IMMA DIE BOUT MINE 5
By Aryanna

A THUGS STREET PRINCESS 3
By Meesha

PRODUCT OF THE STREETS 3
By Demond Money Anderson

CORNER BOYS 2
By Corey Robinson

THE MURDER QUEENS 6&7
By Michael Gallon

CITY OF SMOKE 3
By Molotti

CONFESSIONS OF A DOPE BOY
By Nicholas Lock

THA TAKEOVER
By Keith Chandler

BETRAYAL OF A G 2
By Ray Vinci

CRIME BOSS
By Playa Ray

Available Now

RESTRAINING ORDER 1 & 2
By **CA$H & Coffee**

LOVE KNOWS NO BOUNDARIES 1-3
By **Coffee**

RAISED AS A GOON I, II, III & IV
BRED BY THE SLUMS I, II, III
BLAST FOR ME I & II
ROTTEN TO THE CORE I II III
A BRONX TALE I, II, III
DUFFLE BAG CARTEL I II III IV V VI
HEARTLESS GOON I II III IV V
A SAVAGE DOPEBOY I II
DRUG LORDS I II III
CUTTHROAT MAFIA I II
KING OF THE TRENCHES
By **Ghost**

LAY IT DOWN I & II
LAST OF A DYING BREED I II
BLOOD STAINS OF A SHOTTA I & II III
By **Jamaica**

LOYAL TO THE GAME I II III
LIFE OF SIN I, II III
By **TJ & Jelissa**

IF LOVING HIM IS WRONG…I & II
LOVE ME EVEN WHEN IT HURTS I II III
By **Jelissa**

PUSH IT TO THE LIMIT
By **Bre' Hayes**

FO'EVA ROLLIN' | ASSA RAYMOND BAKER

BLOODY COMMAS I & II
SKI MASK CARTEL I, II & III
KING OF NEW YORK I II, III IV V
RISE TO POWER I II III
COKE KINGS I II III IV V
BORN HEARTLESS I II III IV
KING OF THE TRAP I II
By **T.J. Edwards**

WHEN THE STREETS CLAP BACK I & II III
THE HEART OF A SAVAGE I II III IV
MONEY MAFIA I II
LOYAL TO THE SOIL I II III
By **Jibril Williams**

A DISTINGUISHED THUG STOLE MY HEART I II & III
LOVE SHOULDN'T HURT I II III IV
RENEGADE BOYS 1-4
PAID IN KARMA 1-3
SAVAGE STORMS 1-3
AN UNFORESEEN LOVE 1-3
BABY, I'M WINTERTIME COLD 1-3
A THUG'S STREET PRINCESS 1&2
By **Meesha**

A GANGSTER'S CODE 1-3
A GANGSTER'S SYN 1-3
THE SAVAGE LIFE 1-3
CHAINED TO THE STREETS 1-3
BLOOD ON THE MONEY 1-3
A GANGSTA'S PAIN 1-3
BEAUTIFUL LIES AND UGLY TRUTHS
CHURCH IN THESE STREETS
By **J-Blunt**

CUM FOR ME 1-8
An LDP Erotica Collaboration

BLOOD OF A BOSS 1-5
SHADOWS OF THE GAME
TRAP BASTARD
By **Askari**

THE STREETS BLEED MURDER 1-3
THE HEART OF A GANGSTA 1-3
By **Jerry Jackson**

WHEN A GOOD GIRL GOES BAD
By **Adrienne**

THE COST OF LOYALTY 1-3
By **Kweli**

BRIDE OF A HUSTLA 1-3
THE FETTI GIRLS 1-3
CORRUPTED BY A GANGSTA 1-4
BLINDED BY HIS LOVE
THE PRICE YOU PAY FOR LOVE 1-3
DOPE GIRL MAGIC 1-3
By **Destiny Skai**

A KINGPIN'S AMBITION
A KINGPIN'S AMBITION II
I MURDER FOR THE DOUGH
By **Ambitious**

TRUE SAVAGE 1-7
DOPE BOY MAGIC 1-3
MIDNIGHT CARTEL 1-3
CITY OF KINGZ 1&2
NIGHTMARE ON SILENT AVE
THE PLUG OF LIL MEXICO 1&2
CLASSIC CITY
By **Chris Green**

FO'EVA ROLLIN' | ASSA RAYMOND BAKER

A GANGSTER'S REVENGE 1-4
THE BOSS MAN'S DAUGHTERS 1-5
A SAVAGE LOVE 1&2
BAE BELONGS TO ME 1&2
A HUSTLER'S DECEIT 1-3
WHAT BAD BITCHES DO 1-3
SOUL OF A MONSTER 1-3
KILL ZONE
A DOPE BOY'S QUEEN 1-3
TIL DEATH 1-3
IMMA DIE BOUT MINE 1-4
By **Aryanna**

A DOPEBOY'S PRAYER
By **Eddie "Wolf" Lee**

THE KING CARTEL 1-3
By **Frank Gresham**

THESE NIGGAS AIN'T LOYAL 1-3
By **Nikki Tee**

GANGSTA SHYT 1-3
By **CATO**

THE ULTIMATE BETRAYAL
By **Phoenix**

BOSS'N UP 1-3
By **Royal Nicole**

I LOVE YOU TO DEATH
By **Destiny J**

I RIDE FOR MY HITTA
I STILL RIDE FOR MY HITTA
By **Misty Holt**

FO'EVA ROLLIN' | ASSA RAYMOND BAKER

LOVE & CHASIN' PAPER
By **Qay Crockett**

TO DIE IN VAIN
SINS OF A HUSTLA
By **ASAD**

BROOKLYN HUSTLAZ
By **Boogsy Morina**

BROOKLYN ON LOCK 1 & 2
By **Sonovia**

GANGSTA CITY
By **Teddy Duke**

A DRUG KING AND HIS DIAMOND 1-3
A DOPEMAN'S RICHES
HER MAN, MINE'S TOO 1&2
CASH MONEY HO'S
THE WIFEY I USED TO BE 1&2
PRETTY GIRLS DO NASTY THINGS
By **Nicole Goosby**

LIPSTICK KILLAH 1-3
CRIME OF PASSION 1-3
FRIEND OR FOE 1-3
By **Mimi**

TRAPHOUSE KING 1-3
KINGPIN KILLAZ 1-3
STREET KINGS 1&2
PAID IN BLOOD 1&2
CARTEL KILLAZ 1-3
DOPE GODS 1&2
By **Hood Rich**

THE STREETS ARE CALLING
By **Duquie Wilson**

FO'EVA ROLLIN' | ASSA RAYMOND BAKER

STEADY MOBBN' 1-3
THE STREETS STAINED MY SOUL 1-3
By **Marcellus Allen**

WHO SHOT YA 1-3
SON OF A DOPE FIEND 1-4
HEAVEN GOT A GHETTO 1&2
SKI MASK MONEY 1&2
By **Renta**

GORILLAZ IN THE BAY 1-4
TEARS OF A GANGSTA 1/&2
3X KRAZY 1&2
STRAIGHT BEAST MODE 1&2
By **DE'KARI**

TRIGGADALE 1-3
MURDA WAS THE CASE 1-3
By **Elijah R. Freeman**

SLAUGHTER GANG 1-3
RUTHLESS HEART 1-3
By **Willie Slaughter**

GOD BLESS THE TRAPPERS 1-3
THESE SCANDALOUS STREETS 1-3
FEAR MY GANGSTA 1-5
THESE STREETS DON'T LOVE NOBODY 1-2
BURY ME A G 1-5
A GANGSTA'S EMPIRE 1-4
THE DOPEMAN'S BODYGAURD 1&2
THE REALEST KILLAZ 1-3
THE LAST OF THE OGS 1-3
By **Tranay Adams**

MARRIED TO A BOSS 1-3
By **Destiny Skai & Chris Green**

FO'EVA ROLLIN' | ASSA RAYMOND BAKER

KINGZ OF THE GAME 1-7
CRIME BOSS 1-3
By **Playa Ray**

FUK SHYT
By **Blakk Diamond**

DON'T F#CK WITH MY HEART 1&2
By **Linnea**

ADDICTED TO THE DRAMA 1-3
IN THE ARM OF HIS BOSS
By **Jamila**

LOYALTY AIN'T PROMISED 1&2
By **Keith Williams**

YAYO 1-4
A SHOOTER'S AMBITION 1&2
BRED IN THE GAME
By **S. Allen**

TRAP GOD 1-3
RICH $AVAGE 1-3
MONEY IN THE GRAVE 1-3
CARTEL MONEY
By **Martell Troublesome Bolden**

FOREVER GANGSTA 1&2
GLOCKS ON SATIN SHEETS 1&2
By **Adrian Dulan**

TOE TAGZ 1-4
LEVELS TO THIS SHYT 1&2
IT'S JUST ME AND YOU
By **Ah'Million**

KINGPIN DREAMS 1-3
RAN OFF ON DA PLUG
By **Paper Boi Rari**

THE STREETS MADE ME 1-3
By **Larry D. Wright**

CONFESSIONS OF A GANGSTA 1-4
CONFESSIONS OF A JACKBOY 1-3
CONFESSIONS OF A HITMAN
By **Nicholas Lock**

I'M NOTHING WITHOUT HIS LOVE
SINS OF A THUG
TO THE THUG I LOVED BEFORE
A GANGSTA SAVED XMAS
IN A HUSTLER I TRUST
By **Monet Dragun**

QUIET MONEY 1-3
THUG LIFE 1-3
EXTENDED CLIP 1&2
A GANGSTA'S PARADISE
By **Trai'Quan**

CAUGHT UP IN THE LIFE 1-3
THE STREETS NEVER LET GO 1-3
By **Robert Baptiste**

NEW TO THE GAME 1-3
MONEY, MURDER & MEMORIES 1-3
By **Malik D. Rice**

CREAM 2-3
THE STREETS WILL TALK
By **Yolanda Moore**

THE STREETS WILL NEVER CLOSE 1-3
By **K'ajji**

FO'EVA ROLLIN' | ASSA RAYMOND BAKER

LIFE OF A SAVAGE 1-4
A GANGSTA'S QUR'AN 1-4
MURDA SEASON 1-3
GANGLAND CARTEL 1-3
CHI'RAQ GANGSTAS 1-4
KILLERS ON ELM STREET 1-3
JACK BOYZ N DA BRONX 1-3
A DOPEBOY'S DREAM 1-3
JACK BOYS VS DOPE BOYS 1-3
COKE GIRLZ
COKE BOYS
SOSA GANG 1&2
BRONX SAVAGES
BODYMORE KINGPINS
BLOOD OF A GOON
By **Romell Tukes**

CONCRETE KILLA 1-3
VICIOUS LOYALTY 1-3
By **Kingpen**

THE ULTIMATE SACRIFICE 1-6
KHADIFI
IF YOU CROSS ME ONCE 1-3
ANGEL 1-4
IN THE BLINK OF AN EYE
By **Anthony Fields**

THE LIFE OF A HOOD STAR
By **Ca$h & Rashia Wilson**

NIGHTMARES OF A HUSTLA 1-3
BLOOD AND GAMES 1&2
By **King Dream**

GHOST MOB
By **Stilloan Robinson**

FO'EVA ROLLIN' | ASSA RAYMOND BAKER

HARD AND RUTHLESS 1&2
MOB TOWN 251
THE BILLIONAIRE BENTLEYS 1-3
REAL G'S MOVE IN SILENCE
By **Von Diesel**

MOB TIES 1-7
SOUL OF A HUSTLER, HEART OF A KILLER 1-3
GORILLAZ IN THE TRENCHES
By **SayNoMore**

BODYMORE MURDERLAND 1-3
THE BIRTH OF A GANGSTER 1-4
By **Delmont Player**

FOR THE LOVE OF A BOSS 1&2
By **C. D. Blue**

KILLA KOUNTY 1-5
By **Khufu**

MOBBED UP 1-4
THE BRICK MAN 1-5
THE COCAINE PRINCESS 1-10
STEPPERS 1-3
SUPER GREMLIN 1-4
By **King Rio**

MONEY GAME 1&2
By **Smoove Dolla**

A GANGSTA'S KARMA 1-4
By **FLAME**

KING OF THE TRENCHES 1-3
By **GHOST & TRANAY ADAMS**

FO'EVA ROLLIN' | ASSA RAYMOND BAKER

QUEEN OF THE ZOO 1&2
By **Black Migo**

GRIMEY WAYS 1-3
BETRAYAL OF A G
By **Ray Vinci**

XMAS WITH AN ATL SHOOTER
By **Ca$h & Destiny Skai**

KING KILLA 1&2
By **Vincent "Vitto" Holloway**

BETRAYAL OF A THUG 1&2
By **Fre$h**

THE MURDER QUEENS 1-5
By **Michael Gallon**

FOR THE LOVE OF BLOOD 1-4
By **Jamel Mitchell**

HOOD CONSIGLIERE 1&2
NO TIME FOR ERROR
By **Keese**

PROTÉGÉ OF A LEGEND 1&2
LOVE IN THE TRENCHES 1&2
By **Corey Robinson**

THE PLUG'S RUTHLESS DAUGHTER
By **Tony Daniels**

BORN IN THE GRAVE 1-3
CRIME PAYS
By **Self Made Tay**

MOAN IN MY MOUTH
By **XTASY**

FO'EVA ROLLIN' | ASSA RAYMOND BAKER

TORN BETWEEN A GANGSTER AND A GENTLEMAN
By **J-BLUNT & Miss Kim**

LOYALTY IS EVERYTHING 1-3
CITY OF SMOKE 1&2
By **Molotti**

HERE TODAY GONE TOMORROW 1&2
By **Fly Rock**

WOMEN LIE MEN LIE 1-4
FIFTY SHADES OF SNOW 1-3
STACK BEFORE YOU SPLURGE
GIRLS FALL LIKE DOMINOES
NAÏVE TO THE STREETS
By **ROY MILLIGAN**

PILLOW PRINCESS
By **S. Hawkins**

THE BUTTERFLY MAFIA 1-3
SALUTE MY SAVAGERY 1&2
By **Fumiya Payne**

THE LANE 1&2
By Ken-Ken Spence

THE PUSSY TRAP 1-5
By **Nene Capri**

DIRTY DNA
By **Blaque**

SANCTIFIED AND HORNY
by **XTASY**

BOOKS BY LDP'S CEO, CA$H

TRUST IN NO MAN
TRUST IN NO MAN 2
TRUST IN NO MAN 3
BONDED BY BLOOD
SHORTY GOT A THUG
THUGS CRY
THUGS CRY 2
THUGS CRY 3
TRUST NO BITCH
TRUST NO BITCH 2
TRUST NO BITCH 3
TIL MY CASKET DROPS
RESTRAINING ORDER
RESTRAINING ORDER 2
IN LOVE WITH A CONVICT
LIFE OF A HOOD STAR
XMAS WITH AN ATL SHOOTER